SK

Was the computer game Space Demons real, or was the whole exhilarating, terrifying experience just a dream? For those who played it, the memories are still disturbingly vivid.

There have been several changes during the year that has passed since they solved the riddle of Space Demons. Andrew Hayford now has a stepbrother whom he dislikes. Ben Challis, bullied by his older brother, finds himself struggling with his own feelings of inferiority. Elaine Taylor discovers that living with foster parents is far from easy; and for Mario Ferrone, despite his bravado, life seems to hold little promise.

When Andrew takes possession of the new hypergame Skymaze, the children are lured into a compellingly beautiful but treacherous world where their own fears and problems are chillingly reflected . . . and where anything, but anything, can happen!

This book is for everyone who asked for a sequel.

SKYMAZE

Gillian Rubinstein

MAMMOTH

Lyrics from the song "La Bamba" are reproduced with the
permission of EMI Music Publishing Australia

First published 1989 by Omnibus Books
in association with Penguin Books, Australia
First published in Great Britain 1990 by Mammoth
an imprint of Mandarin Paperbacks
Michelin House, 81 Fulham Road, London SW3 6RB

Mandarin is an imprint of the Octopus Publishing Group

ISBN 0 7497 0397 0

A CIP catalogue record for this title
is available from the British Library

Printed in Great Britain
by Cox & Wyman Ltd, Reading, Berkshire

Also by Gillian Rubinstein in Mammoth

Beyond the Labyrinth
Space Demons

This work was assisted by a writer's fellowship from the Australia Council, the Federal Government's arts funding and advisory body.

CHAPTER ONE

When Ben Challis walked into the deli over the road from Fernleigh High School one afternoon in August, Mario Ferrone was already in there playing a coin-op game, watched admiringly by his brother John and, less admiringly, by Elaine Taylor.

Ben bought himself a Mars bar and went over to join them. "How come you never wear school uniform?" he said to Mario, who was in his usual black jeans and black jacket.

Mario did not reply, but John answered for him. "He doesn't like school uniform," he explained.

"I don't like it either," Ben grumbled, his eyes on the screen, where the score was reaching undreamed of heights. "But if I don't wear it I get into trouble. What I want to know is, how come he gets away with it?"

"Shut up!" Mario said. He swore as he lost his last life and the game came to an end. "You're always gabbling on about something, Challis," he said in disgust. "Look what you made me do." He entered his name as champion player. It was already there in second, third and fourth place. "Give us another forty cents," he ordered John.

John obediently handed over two twenty-cent coins.

1

Elaine said, rather scornfully, "Well, I'm not hanging around here any longer. I'll see you all later."

Mario pocketed the coins. "I'll walk along with you." He gave the machine a kick. "This is a dumb game anyway. It's too easy. Has anyone got any money? I'm starving."

Ben found he couldn't help saying, "I've got a couple of dollars."

"Get us a Mars bar, then. Oh, and a Coke!"

Wondering why he should, but still doing it, Ben bought them for him and then followed the others up the street. Elaine had walked away swiftly, and he had to run to catch up. She watched in disgust as Mario gave his bike to John to wheel and took the bar and the drink.

"You are such a bully," she accused him, and then she said witheringly to Ben and John, "Why the heck do you let him boss you around like that?"

"I don't boss them around," Mario replied carelessly. "I look after them. I don't let anyone else boss them around. So they're grateful to me, aren't you, guys?" He dropped the empty Coke can on the ground and gave it a vigorous kick that sent it flying across the road. Then he took out a packet of cigarettes and lit one. Blowing out the smoke, he said to Ben, "This isn't the way to your place."

"He can walk this way if he wants to," Elaine said, exasperated.

"See you tomorrow," Mario said pointedly to Ben.

"Yeah, well, I have to get home anyway," Ben said. "I've got some things to do." He couldn't immediately think of any, but he didn't feel like tagging along with the others if he wasn't wanted. Elaine made an angry noise with her tongue and shook her head at him. Mario ignored him. Only John, struggling behind them trying to push two bikes at once, gave him a friendly grin and said, "See you!"

Ben walked home feeling vaguely irritated with himself because he knew he had been taken advantage of yet again. He hoped his parents were home, but as usual the garage was empty and the house was quiet. He walked up the driveway and round to the back. Both his parents were teachers. His mother was deputy principal of a primary school in a disadvantaged area, and his father was a maths and physics teacher at a high school in the southern suburbs. They were both heavily involved in school affairs and extra-mural activities, with the result that for weeks on end Ben only saw them in passing. His older brother, Darren, was meant to keep an eye on him, but with Darren, that was more like being under surveillance.

He was standing outside the back door, feeling in his pocket for his key, when he heard a sudden rustle that made him jump. Before he could move, a hand reached through the ivy-covered trellis along the side of the house and grabbed him.

"Hunter!" Darren hissed at him through the foliage.

"Get lost, Darren!" Ben cried angrily. "I've been hassled all day. I'm not in the mood for your dumb games!"

Once, it seemed like a long time ago, the game of Hunter had been fun, something he had been happy to play with an older brother he liked and admired. He had even been flattered that Darren wanted to play with him, and he would have agreed to anything that included him in Darren's life. Now he wasn't sure he wanted to be included any more. The once innocent game had turned into something much more sinister and unpleasant. Ben didn't like it, and he didn't like what Darren was turning into, either. Their relationship had got stuck in a pattern that neither of them seemed able to break out of. Darren was always the pursuer and the victor. Ben was the quarry and the victim.

Darren made up the rules to the game, and sometimes it went on for days. Ben never knew when Darren was going to make the final "kill", but it was usually when there was no one else around to see, and it involved various sophisticated forms of torture such as can only be dreamed up by the seventeen-year-old male mind.

"Come on," Darren ordered. "I've been studying hard all day and I need some relaxation. You've got to get back to the house, otherwise you're dead."

"Aww, Darren!" Ben pleaded. He tried to wriggle out of Darren's grasp and succeeded only in scratching his hand on the trellis.

"Would you rather just stay here?" Darren enquired conversationally, looking as if he would be quite happy to stay in that position for some hours.

"I need to go to the dunny!" Ben exclaimed.

"I'll let you go if you promise to play, you little wimp!"

Ben gave in, as he had known he would all along. "There must be something wrong with me," he castigated himself, as he went to the toilet. "Why don't I just say no!" He washed his hands quickly and then stood listening at the bathroom door, wondering where Darren was. If he was still outside the back door, Ben could let himself out the front and get away. He was tiptoeing down the passageway when he heard a creak from the kitchen. He sped down to the front door, opened it, and dashed down the steps as quietly as he could.

Darren was crouching behind the brush fence,

having run around the side of the house as Ben was coming through it. He loomed up beside Ben like a zombie and hissed in his ear, "I'll give you five minutes' start!"

"Okay!" Ben shouted rather desperately at him. Reluctantly, he began to run down Forsyth Avenue. He had a stack of homework to do, and he wanted to watch television too, and instead he was running round the streets, pursued by the maniac who called himself his brother! "You are a moron," he told himself. But he didn't stop running.

As always, the game began to exert its hold over him. His heart began to thump, not only from the running, and his breath was rasping in his throat. It was so easy for him to imagine that he really was being pursued, that it really was a matter of life and death. He sometimes felt that he had inside him a reservoir of fears that didn't usually bother him, but that came oozing out from time to time, especially when he was playing Hunter. Nightmares that he would have preferred to forget, of being chased, cornered and devoured by monsters with human faces, surfaced to haunt him. The quiet suburban streets and tidy gardens looked faintly distorted, as though he was in a dream, and even the stobie poles loomed in a peculiar and threatening way.

He came to a corner and slowed down to peer cautiously round it. The streets were empty, and the fading light was starting to drain the colour from the leafless trees and the winter gardens. The sky was grey and overcast, slightly dappled towards the west. It was not particularly cold, but there was something bleak and cheerless about the afternoon that made Ben shiver. He wished he was indoors in the light and the warmth.

Across the road he could see the lighted windows of Andrew Hayford's house. The brilliant idea came to him that he could duck in there and hide out for an hour or so. With any luck Darren would get fed up with looking for him out in the streets and Ben could get home safe. By then his parents might be home too. It wouldn't put an end to this game of Hunter, but it would certainly postpone it for a bit.

He took a swift look round the street but couldn't spot Darren anywhere. He ran quickly up to the Hayfords' front door and rang the bell.

There was an air of chaos about the usually impeccable house, and when Andrew's mother opened the door, Ben thought she looked quite different, younger and more animated.

"Hi, Benny!" she greeted him warmly, and she even laid her arm across his shoulder in a sort of hug. He had grown a few centimetres since he had last seen her, he realised, and now he was nearly as tall as she was. He wasn't sure whether he was expected to hug back or not, so he stood there rather awkwardly until she let him go. She gave him a radiantly happy smile. "We haven't seen you for ages," she exclaimed. "Excuse the mess, won't you? The removalists are coming tomorrow!" Then she skipped on to the first step and called up the stairs, "Andrew! Ben's here!"

Andrew appeared on the top landing. "Hi! You can come and help me pack!"

Ben took the stairs two at a time, still thinking about the Benny and the sort of hug. He knew Andrew's mother had recently married again. It seemed to be suiting her, but he wondered how much the new situation was suiting Andrew.

"I didn't realise you were moving so soon," he said. "How's it all going?"

Andrew pushed the door of his bedroom shut behind them and made an awesomely revolting face at it. "Dreadful! This has to be the low point of my life." He picked up a pile of clothes and slung them into a half-full packing case. Then he slid a row of books off the bookshelf and threw them in on top. "At least things can only get better from now on," he said, forcing a grin. "Can't they?"

"Live in hope!" Ben said.

"Oh, you know me. Mr Optimism himself." But Andrew did not look like Mr Optimism as he gloomily surveyed the wreck of his room. Ben followed his gaze. The once beautifully decorated and furnished room looked as if a bomb had hit it. There were three half-filled packing cases under the window and two empty ones by the door. Every available surface, including the floor, had something piled on it.

"I wish I could just chuck it all away," Andrew remarked. "It'd be better than packing it all up."

"You can give it to me," Ben suggested. "I'll look after the cars and the Lego for you, and the *Mad* magazines."

"Done!" Andrew replied. "Start packing them up!"

"When are you moving?"

"The van's coming tomorrow morning. Tonight's our last night here."

"Cheer up. We can still see each other," Ben said. He was feeling a little bit guilty for not having seen more of Andrew lately now that the family was moving to a new house in North Adelaide, where Andrew's stepfather, Dr Keith Freeman, would have his rooms. The two boys had been best friends since kindergarten, but now that they were at different secondary

7

schools they were beginning to drift apart. Ben went to Fernleigh, the local high school, but Andrew's parents had wanted to send him to a private college on the other side of the city. Ben and Andrew had been such exclusive friends that without Andrew Ben had found quite a gap in his life, which hanging round with Mario and John Ferrone at school did not really fill. But sometimes it seemed to him that he was turning into a different sort of person from what he and everyone else had thought he was, and it was hard to make friends when you didn't know what you were going to turn out like.

"Thanks for those comforting words," Andrew said. "I suppose it's not the other end of the earth. Actually, I'm going to need all the friends I can get. I shall probably be camping on your doorstep five nights a week, begging you to give me political asylum."

"It won't be that bad," Ben said, trying to sound reassuring.

Andrew gave him a dark and totally unconvinced look. "Oh, won't it! I keep thinking that I could handle bits of it at a time. It's just trying to handle the whole lot at once that worries me. Like, I could handle Mum getting married to Keith if we didn't have to move. And I could handle moving if it didn't mean moving into the same house as Paul Freeman. And I could handle Paul Freeman if I didn't have to see him at school every day. And so on. Et cetera."

"What's he like?"

"Paul or Keith?"

"Well, Paul mainly. But Keith too."

"Keith's okay, really, though I couldn't stand him when I first met him, and I still find some things about him hard to take. Like he's always asking me what I'm really feeling, and what exactly I mean by that remark.

8

Half the time I don't know anyway. And when I tell him I don't know, he tells me what I really feel and what exactly I meant." Andrew took off an imaginary pair of glasses and waved them in the air. "You're feeling *insecure*, Andy. You need to be reassured that we all still care for you."

"Do you?" Ben asked with interest.

"How the hell would I know?" Andrew replied with a deep sigh that was only partly assumed. "It's all too confusing for me." He was silent for a few moments as he emptied the contents of the top drawer of his chest out on to the floor and sifted through them. "I guess I feel isolated mainly," he said finally. "The way things used to be, it was as if I was in the centre of everything, and now it's like the centre has moved away. It's gone somewhere else and I can't find it. And I'm definitely not in it any more."

"What about Paul?"

"I just don't like him," Andrew replied shortly. "He's one of those people you'd have absolutely nothing to do with normally, and then you find yourself living in the same family. And everyone says idiotic things like, 'Oh, how nice for you to have an older brother.'"

"As if anyone in their right mind would choose to have an older brother," Ben said with feeling. "How old is he?"

"Just old enough to be a nuisance. It'd be okay if he was heaps older and in the Senior School, but he's in Second Year, and you know what they're like!"

"No Second Year dares hassle us!" Ben said rather smugly. "They'd have to answer to Mars if they did." He preferred not to think about the price Mario exacted for his protection.

"Yeah, it's all very well for you. Sometimes I wish I was at Fernleigh too. I wouldn't mind having a Mario

Ferrone looking out for me. I think Mario would make a very useful bodyguard." Andrew sighed again. He finished emptying one drawer of the chest and started on another. Everything looked old and messy, and he was sure there was nothing there he really wanted to keep. He tipped the contents into a green garbage bag that was already almost overflowing. It wobbled sideways, and most of the things Andrew had just tipped in fell out again on to the floor.

"Gee, I'm never going to get this done," he said hopelessly, trying to pick everything up at once.

It was so unlike Andrew to sound hopeless that Ben looked across at him in concern. "Do you want me to help?"

"You can help with the packing. I'm not sure anyone can help with Paul!"

"Well, what exactly does he do?" Ben put down the magazine he had been skimming through, and started to arrange all the magazines in a neat pile.

"Oh, you know, just your usual sort of all-purpose hassling." Andrew sounded rather distant, as though he had started thinking about something else. Ben glanced up from the magazines and saw he was looking at a scrappy old piece of paper. In his other hand was an empty case with purple and black writing on it. He felt Ben's gaze upon him and looked up. The boys' eyes met. Andrew laughed and waved the case.

"Do you remember this, my man?"

There was a moment's silence, a beat, and then Ben said casually, "Yeah, that was quite a good game. What happened to it? Did you erase it by mistake?"

"What are you talking about?" Andrew demanded incredulously. "You know perfectly well what happened. You were there. You played it."

"Yes, I know I played it. Like I said, it was quite a

10

good game."

"That's not quite how I'd describe it," Andrew said with feeling. "Don't you remember what actually happened? Don't you remember Space Demons?"

To him the whole game was still vividly alive. He could recall the exact details of its colours and sounds. They made him shiver with excitement and terror. He realised that just thinking about it made him feel less hopeless. On reflection, the terror of the game seemed nothing beside the excitement. He could remember exactly how it had felt to be a demon hunter, when you got into the game and actually played it from the inside. It felt a lot better than being a First Year student at a new school he didn't much like, being hassled by a new stepbrother he didn't like at all.

Ben had a different set of memories. He had blotted out large chunks of the time they had all played Space Demons. Remembering it now made him feel extremely uncomfortable. He had no intention of letting Andrew embroil him in anything like that again. And besides, he really was not sure how much of it had been real, and how much had been simply their imaginations running wild.

"You were going through a pretty crazy time last year, you know," he told Andrew. "You were imagining some weird stuff. Everyone thought you were going nuts."

"Mario didn't!"

"What would he know? He's totally and utterly insane himself. You wouldn't have had anything to do with him if you hadn't been going mad too."

"I can't have imagined the whole thing, though," Andrew said stubbornly.

"Why not? You were obsessed with computer games, you were going through a tough time, you

11

escaped into a fantasy. People do it all the time," Ben replied. "You see them on the buses talking to themselves!"

"What about this, then?" Andrew held up the piece of paper. "This is the address to send off to for the next game. Don't you remember, the game wiped itself out because we got through it successfully. And then this address came up on the screen, and Mario told me to write it down. You must remember. We were all here in this room. Elaine Taylor was here too. There's the computer!"

Ben looked across at the blank screen. It looked too innocent now ever to have been the source of such menace. "Why didn't you send off for it then?" he countered.

"I was going to, but then there was too much else going on. All the fuss about the divorce, and then Dad getting tied up with Rose in Sydney, and Mum going all swimmy-eyed over Keith, and then starting at St Hugh's. I kept meaning to send off for it, but it never seemed to be quite the right time."

"There you are," Ben said triumphantly. "That proves it. You never sent off for it because you know at some deep level that there's not going to be anything unusual about it. You'd rather hang on to your fantasy than test it and find it's untrue."

"What a load of crap!" Andrew replied. "Where do you get all these phoney ideas from? You're as bad as Keith!"

"Dad's doing a counselling course. It tells you a lot about people's ulterior motives. It's really neat!"

"Huh!" Andrew dismissed the counselling course with a snort of contempt. "You're absolutely wrong. And just to prove how wrong you are, I think I'll send off for the new game." He didn't sound hopeless any more. He was grinning with delight. The idea cheered him up immensely. "It's just what I need to take my mind off my unbearable circumstances." He stretched over to the next drawer of the chest, and pulled it open. "There should be some writing paper in here somewhere. I'm going to send off for it right now!"

Ben straightened up the stack of magazines with a vague feeling of foreboding. "You're going to be disappointed," he warned. "It'll only be an ordinary game."

"Then you won't mind coming over to play it, will you?" Andrew replied. "Come on, let's get the rest of the stuff packed up. Then we can burn down to the Post Office."

"Okay," Ben agreed, but only because it seemed marginally preferable to playing Hunter in the streets with Darren. All the same, he had an uncomfortable feeling he was getting out of the frying pan and into the fire.

CHAPTER TWO

A few weeks had passed and Andrew had settled into the house in North Adelaide before the package arrived. His mother mentioned it in the car on their way home from school. "Something came for you from Japan today, Andrew."

Zing! His whole body thrilled in excitement, as though he had touched an electric current.

Paul, who was in the front seat, turned round. "What is it?" he asked jealously.

"Always shoving his big nose into things," Andrew thought with dislike. Paul's nose was rather big, and he was very inquisitive. Everything Andrew did fascinated him, although he pretended to ignore him, and any secret Andrew had Paul always ferreted out. He also kept a strict balance sheet on the way the two parents treated the stepbrothers, and was very quick to draw attention to anything he thought unfair or any way he thought Andrew was being favoured.

Since the death of his mother when he was six, Paul had grown unusually close to his father, and he viewed with some alarm Andrew's intrusion into their lives. On the whole he did not mind his father's remarriage; he liked Andrew's mother, and he had to admit it was

14

pleasant to have a woman in the house again, after their rather spartan male existence. He just thought it was a great shame that Andrew had to be part of the package, especially since Andrew's confident and charming manner was quite unlike Paul's own rather intense and introverted personality.

"I don't know yet, do I?" Andrew replied guardedly.

"Is it some sort of present?" Paul insisted. "Who paid for it?"

"None of your business," Andrew retorted rudely.

"Oh, isn't it?" Paul glared at Andrew over the back of the seat. "I just might make it my business."

"Boys," Marjorie pleaded as she pulled up outside the house, thinking in despair that Paul could start an argument over anything.

"Give us the key, Mum, I'll open the door for you." Andrew took it from her and sprinted up the path to the front door, where he rapidly tapped in the digits to deactivate the burglar alarm, and put the key in the lock.

"You can help me with the shopping," Marjorie said firmly to Paul, who was preparing to pursue him. She didn't really think it was any of Paul's business either, and though she tried very hard to be fair to him at other times, she thought this time she would give Andrew a head start.

By the time Paul had reluctantly carried in the shopping and helped Marjorie put it away, Andrew was safely locked in his room. He looked at the packet carefully. He didn't want to miss any important clues. It was a padded bag with his address typed on the label, and some rather ordinary Japanese stamps. No indication of the sender; nothing else that seemed of any significance. He opened the bag very carefully, and drew out the disc. Then he ran his fingers round

15

the inside of the bag to make sure there was no accompanying message. It was quite empty.

He turned his attention to the disc, barely noticing that his pulse was starting to speed up, and his fingers were tingling.

Across the top of the case ran the title of the game. SKYMAZE.

Andrew spoke the word aloud in high satisfaction. Below it was a picture that he recognised instantly. It was a black sky studded with silver stars, and below it was the faint impression of a cliff top. Andrew grinned like a maniac as he remembered the last time he had seen that cliff top and those stars. The game must be a continuation of Space Demons. It started from the place where Space Demons ended. Peering at the sky, he could see a sort of network that connected the cliff top with the stars.

Skymaze!

He couldn't wait to play it. He would show Ben that it was not just an ordinary game. His heart was jumping with excitement, and his eyes were gleaming. Life was definitely improving!

There was only one problem—where was he going to play it? He thought with a flash of bitterness of his old house, where he had the computer all to himself in his own room where he could lock the door. Now, because he had to share it with Paul, the computer was kept in a study off the family room at the back of the house. There was no way Andrew could use it in private—and if Skymaze was anything like Space Demons, privacy was what he was going to need.

He was still thinking about the problem when the door handle rattled and Paul's voice called, "Hey, Andrew!"

"What do you want?"

"You want to have a game of pool?" Paul's voice sounded unusually friendly, and this made Andrew suspicious at once. "He probably only wants me to play so he can find out what was in the parcel," he thought. "Darn it, how am I going to get to play this game without anyone seeing?"

"No thanks," he said back through the closed door.

There was a moment's silence during which Andrew hoped fervently that Paul was removing himself, but then the older boy remarked, "I'll tell Dad you vetoed."

Andrew swore to himself. This was one of Keith's plans for Happy Family living. No one was allowed to refuse a reasonable request or suggestion from another member of the family. If you did, you were using the veto, which was the same as rejecting the other person and refusing to recognise their right to exist and their right to relate to you. "We have to learn to say yes to each other, not to say no," Keith explained to Andrew. Sometimes it could be an excellent rule, like when the boys suggested to Keith that he should take them to a movie or out for dinner, but Andrew wasn't so keen on it when it involved Paul.

"I've got to do my homework," he said, not quite truthfully.

"Ha ha!" Paul replied. "You can do it later. Just a short game. I've got homework too, and then I'm going to have a game of squash with Dad."

"Great!" Andrew thought with satisfaction. "They'll be out for an hour at least. I can get on the computer then."

"Okay," he conceded. He hid the disc under his pillow, and opened the door.

The two boys descended the stairs and walked down

17

the corridor to the back of the house. It was a large nineteenth-century mansion with spacious rooms and wrought-iron verandas, surrounded by small, formal grounds and protected by a complex electronic security system. Andrew could see that it was gracious and beautiful, but privately he rather disliked it. It was too stately and dignified, and too dark inside. He preferred his old house, and he had liked living in the foothills. North Adelaide felt like the middle of the city. He was thinking about this with half his mind as he followed Paul to the games room. The other half was still busy with Skymaze.

The games room was under the house, in what had been a summer parlour. It had a decorated ceiling, and its windows looked out on to the garden, where the flower beds were at eye level and the shrubs gave a greenish light to the room.

"I didn't know you knew anyone in Japan," Paul observed, selecting a cue and chalking it.

"My father has some friends over there," Andrew replied non-committally, setting out the balls and mentally congratulating himself on being right about Paul's ulterior motives. "Are we playing pool or snooker?"

"Pool. I'll let you break. Nice friends to send you presents."

Andrew did not reply. He removed the triangle from the pool balls and prepared to break. It was a lucky shot: two balls rolled gently into the top pocket.

"Hey, look at that," he crowed. "Ace shot!"

"Fluke," Paul sneered.

"No fluke," Andrew contradicted him, promptly sinking another ball. "I just happen to be a brilliant pool player. You should know that by now. Are we playing for money?"

"No, we're not playing for money, you mercenary

18

little beggar. We're playing for pure brotherly love. Nice, isn't it?" Paul took his turn, got two balls down, and then missed an easy shot. "What was in the parcel?"

"What's it matter to you?" Andrew said, concentrating on the shot.

"Why're you being so secretive?" Paul countered, chalking his cue again elaborately.

Andrew was on the eight ball by now. "Don't bother chalking," he said. "The game's over!" The eight ball disappeared with a satisfying clunk.

Andrew turned to Paul with a grin of triumph, and caught the look of frustrated anger on his stepbrother's face. "Gee, he hates to lose," Andrew thought. "But what am I supposed to do? I'm not going to lose on purpose just so he can feel good. It's not my fault that I'm better at pool than he is."

"You want to play again?" he asked, expecting Paul to say no.

"Okay," Paul said. "My break. But let's play for something this time. If I win, you have to show me the present you got."

"All right," said Andrew. "And if I win, you have to shut up about it for ever." It seemed like a sure thing. Nine times out of ten he beat Paul at pool. But on his second shot he hit the 10 too hard. It ricocheted on to the eight ball and sent it into the pocket.

"My game," Paul said evilly.

Andrew swore. "Come on," he said. "That was just bad luck, you know it was. Put the eight ball back and we'll play on."

"No way." Paul gave an exaggerated laugh of indignation. "We made a deal. You lost the game. Now you show me what was in the package."

Andrew felt strongly that he was morally in the

19

right, enough to make a stand on it. "Well, I'm not going to," he retorted. "You can get stuffed." He put his cue back in the rack and turned to walk out of the room.

Paul grabbed him by the arm. "You little creep," he hissed in Andrew's face. "You're so darned arrogant. I'd like to teach you a lesson!"

"Let go of me," Andrew yelled angrily. He wrenched his arm away from Paul's grip but somehow in his rage the pulling away turned into a pushing towards and he found himself smacking Paul on the nose.

Paul grunted in surprise and anger, and smacked Andrew back hard on the side of the head. Then he stood there, hands still raised, as if daring Andrew to retaliate. Neither boy was particularly fond of fighting, but Andrew was enraged enough to risk another punch, socking Paul this time in the ribs. Paul clipped him over the ear again.

It was still not really a fight, more like slow-motion sparring, neither of them wanting to go over the top and completely out of control, when they were interrupted by a cheerful shout from above. "Paul, Andy! Are you down there?" and Dr Keith Freeman came leaping boyishly down the stairs.

The two boys jumped apart, but there was nothing they could do to disguise the violent atmosphere. Keith's cheerful face lengthened noticeably as he looked from one to the other.

"Paul, please tell me how you are feeling at the moment?" he enquired, trying to sound patient.

"I feel Andrew is a conceited creep and a cheat!" Paul responded furiously.

"Ask me how I feel!" Andrew exclaimed. "I feel Paul is a bully and a snoop." The two boys glared at each other.

"You're bound to have hostile and negative feelings towards each other," Keith said reassuringly. "It's perfectly natural. But it's against house rules to express these feelings violently."

"I was trying to be friendly," Paul said with disgusted virtue. "I asked him to have a game of pool. And when he lost he wouldn't keep the deal."

"Is that a true version of the facts, Andy?"

"Not really," Andrew said, wishing for the hundredth time that Keith wouldn't call him Andy. "He only asked me to play so he could worm something out of me. It's a secret, and I don't want him to know about it."

"You can share secrets with us, Andy. We're your family now. You don't need to keep things to yourself so much. You can trust us. When you won't tell Paul things, he feels rejected by you—"

"That's right!" Paul put in swiftly.

"—and that's no way to build a trusting relationship. I know it's not easy for you and I know it's going to take time. But we all live in the same house now—we have to sort things out." Keith nodded two or three times to himself at the end of this speech, and smiled at the boys. Then he put his arms round them both and gave them a hug. "You are both terrific people," he said. "I know you're going to come to appreciate each other. Now, what about that game of squash?"

"You're on," Paul said.

"Andy?"

"I've got something else I want to do right now," Andrew said, disentangling himself from the hug, and retreating up the stairs. He could feel his stepfather's eyes on him, and knew just the sort of quizzical, concerned look that would be on his face. It didn't

21

make him feel any better to hear Paul say, as he reached the hallway, "That's just typical of Andrew, Dad. He's not even trying to be part of us."

"I don't want to be part of you," Andrew muttered to himself as he raced up the stairs. "I just want to be on my own and play Skymaze."

Andrew's room was at the side of the house, over an extension that had been added as a garage. He heard the doors open, and he watched Keith's white Lancia back out and disappear at speed in the direction of the Leisure Centre, where the Freemans would play a few games of squash, and no doubt take a turn in the sauna and the spa. Then he took the disc out from under his pillow and went quietly down the stairs, his footsteps muffled by the thick carpet, and into the study. He switched the computer on and put the disc in. He took a deep breath and typed in RUN SKYMAZE.

He held the joystick with fingers that trembled slightly. The computer screen gave a flicker. Letters began to print themselves rapidly across the screen.

WELCOME TO THE HYPERGAME SKYMAZE. YOU ARE WARNED NOT TO ATTEMPT THIS GAME IF YOU HAVE NOT MASTERED THE PREVIOUS GAME IN THE SERIES, SPACE DEMONS.

That was all. No further instructions followed. Andrew read the message through again, and since nothing else happened, he experimentally pressed the fire button on the joystick. The screen cleared. Its original blue colour darkened to almost black. One by one silver stars appeared as though in the night sky, above a cliff. It was a scene that was exhilaratingly familiar, one that Andrew had dreamed about often and longed to be able to return to. With mounting excitement he peered at the stars.

When he looked closely at them they seemed to be unconnected to anything else, but when he glanced away again, with his peripheral vision he could see the faintest of lines running like a web between them. He pressed the fire button again, and a small figure came on to the screen. He studied it closely. It had a very familiar look about it, and after a few seconds it dawned on him who it was. It was himself, a perfect tiny image of Andrew Hayford.

He exhaled sharply. Seeing his own image moving on the screen, controlled by the joystick, not only made him identify totally with it, but also promised something much more, something really extraordinary. With the strong sensation that anything, but anything, might be about to happen, Andrew moved the image to the edge of the cliff and then made it jump up on to one of the web lines. The first couple of times it missed and landed back on the cliff again, but the third time it connected with the strand and stayed there. The next time Andrew moved the joystick, the screen changed. The figure moved into the Skymaze.

At the same time, numbers appeared at the sides of the screen. There were two sets. On the left the numbers started at 600 and began to count down. On the right they started at 1 and went up with each screen change.

The background lightened until it was the colour of the dawn sky. With every new screen its hue changed, but always the colours were sky colours, predominantly grey and blue, but occasionally the yellow of sunrise or the pink and green of a stormy sunset. The game seemed to consist of exploring the different levels of the maze. It spiralled away both vertically and horizontally, and every time the screen changed, the score went up. There were ladders to climb that looked as if they were made of delicate steel and swayed dangerously, as though high altitude winds howled through them; there were ropes that he could jump and cling to, swing sideways on or clamber up; tunnels to slide down or crawl through; bridges across deep chasms; cliffs and walkways that crumbled as he traversed them. There were also a number of other hazards that looked innocent but turned out to be lethal when he touched them, like some flowers at the end of a bridge, and some beautiful drops that fell like rain and zapped him when he swung through them.

Andrew marvelled at the complexity of the game, the stunningly realistic graphics and the inventiveness of the different screens. He had lost a couple of lives and been through twenty different levels when the numbers on the left-hand side of the screen came to zero, and the game returned to the original image of the cliff top beneath the starry sky.

"Time limit," he said to himself. "I wonder if you can extend it in any way. I wonder if there's anything to collect."

He set out again, entering the Skymaze through another strand. It was a little harder, and his score was only 15 when he lost his third life by falling too far off a crumbling cliff, and the game ended. He made a mental note of the number of lives, wondered if there was anything he could do to extend them, and started again.

The third route he tried was the most difficult. This time he lost three lives, and the game came to an end with only twelve levels on the score. Yet this route was the most fascinating, with seemingly impossible screens that he was sure could be solved if he practised enough. The game was totally addictive, even at this level, and always at the back of his mind was the spine-tingling thought that at any moment reality might alter and he might find himself actually in the game, playing it from the inside, as he had in Space Demons.

"Unreal!" he thought. "It's so brilliant! But I mustn't be impatient. I must take it slowly. I must learn as much as I can first. That way there won't be any danger. I'm not going to let it get out of hand, like Space Demons nearly did."

All the same, he was confident he could handle it. After all, he had mastered Space Demons.

He was so completely absorbed in the game that he did not hear his mother coming down the passage. She opened the door and came in, making him jump, and making the little figure on the screen miss the rope it was leaping for and plunge downwards through some very realistic clouds. He frowned as he realised that the long fall had killed it.

"Andrew!" Marjorie exclaimed. "I've been looking all over the house for you. Didn't you hear me calling?"

"No, sorry," he said, not looking at her, starting the game again.

A concerned expression came into her face. "Is that a new game?" she demanded anxiously, putting her hand on his shoulder and leaning over the screen.

Andrew gave a deep sigh, removed the disc, and turned the computer off. There was no point risking disappearing under his mother's eyes.

"I'll stop for a bit now," he said.

Marjorie looked relieved. "Good! It's just as well not to get too obsessed with these games. I got quite worried about you last year, do you remember? You wouldn't stop playing that one your father brought back from Japan. What was it called?"

"Space Demons," Andrew said after a pause.

"That's right! I knew it was something dreadful like

25

that." Then she put two and two together, as Andrew had feared she would. "I suppose this one's from your father too, is it?"

"Not exactly," Andrew said. He did not like the way she always now said "your father", as though his father was nothing to do with her any more. His father often did send him things, postcards from wherever he happened to be at the time, and unexpected parcels. But the address was always written by Rose, his girlfriend, and Andrew often privately wondered if his father thought about him much any more at all.

"Is that what was in that parcel from Japan?"

"Yes." Why didn't everybody mind their own business in this house!

"Oh dear!" Marjorie didn't seem to like the sound of it too much. "What's this one called?"

"Skymaze," Andrew replied reluctantly.

"I thought you'd gone off them," Marjorie said. "You've hardly played at all lately."

"No," Andrew thought. "After Space Demons your average computer game seems pretty tame."

"I've been too busy adjusting to circumstances," he said ironically. "Anyway, I'm not going to play any more for now."

"I hope you'll share it with Paul," Marjorie said. There was a pleading note in her voice.

"She's heard about the fight," Andrew thought. "She thinks this would be a good way to make it up, if I offer to let Paul have a shot at the game. But I can't let him, and anyway, I don't want her to keep thinking she's got to pull the strings all the time. If we aren't going to get on, she's not going to be able to make us pretend we are."

"I don't see why I should," he said shortly.

"Oh, Andrew," she said in disappointment. "You

26

mustn't be selfish with your things."

"I don't mind with anything else," Andrew said, trying to sound generous and reasonable, "but he mustn't play Skymaze."

He was adamant about it over the next few days. It didn't go down very well. His mother and stepfather thought he was being childish and unreasonable, and Paul made an issue of it. The relationship between the two boys worsened dramatically from mutual dislike into overt hostility. It made things very unpleasant for everyone at home, and it made school for Andrew nearly unbearable. And all the time his irritation was exacerbated by his intense desire to play Skymaze again. He was obsessed by it, but he was not going to risk playing it when Paul was around.

"I think it's time to seek asylum," he thought one afternoon. "I'd better escape to Ben's place. I'll phone him up and invite myself over, and with any luck I can get to play the game on their computer. I'll never get a chance here!"

He had stayed close to home all week, waiting for the opportunity to get on the computer, but Paul had stayed close to home too, determined either to play the new game as well, or to prevent Andrew playing it. By the end of the week both Keith and Marjorie had ceased to feel sorry for the boys and were simply fed up with them. They thought it was a very good idea when Andrew asked if he could go to Ben's, and Keith suggested that Paul could find a friend to stay with too while he and Marjorie had a weekend away together in the Hills.

Andrew's parents dropped him off outside Ben's house on Saturday morning, and he watched them get back into the car after saying goodbye to him and telling him they would pick him up on Sunday afternoon. He frowned a little in annoyance as his stepfather kissed his mother before starting up the Lancia and driving away. He felt as if they were shutting him out of something, leaving him behind as they escaped to a life in which he had no part. He didn't like to think of them being two separate adult people who were married. It was discomforting and almost embarrassing.

"But I've got Skymaze!" he consoled himself. "And with any luck today I'm going to be able to get into it."

As soon as they were in Ben's room, Andrew took Skymaze out of his overnight bag. "I brought the new game with me," he said, showing it to Ben. "Can we play it on your computer? I never get a chance to use ours any more."

"Now you know what it's like to have an older brother," Ben said, not very sympathetically. "That's been my problem all these years. You'd think that now Darren's doing Matric he wouldn't have time to go on the computer."

"Or play dumb games with me," he added to himself, but he did not mention the games of Hunter aloud. He had never told anyone else about them, as though he was in some way ashamed of them.

Obsessed with the game, Andrew did not notice his silence. "We'll be able to play this, though, won't we? After all, that's the main reason I came."

"Didn't you want to come and see me?"

"Well, sure, but . . . you know!" Andrew gave Ben a disarming grin.

"What's it like?" Ben asked suspiciously, taking the game from Andrew and studying the case.

"It's okay," Andrew said. "And quite harmless. You could be right, you know. It could be just an ordinary game. I mean, I haven't had a lot of time to play it, but so far nothing peculiar's happened. It's just what it says, a skymaze. You see how much of it you can get through before your time runs out. Nothing very special, but the graphics are great and it's kind of addictive."

They went to Ben's parents' study, which was where the computer was kept, and Ben put the game in. He frowned as he read the warning message: WELCOME TO THE HYPERGAME SKYMAZE. YOU ARE WARNED NOT TO ATTEMPT THIS GAME IF YOU HAVE NOT MASTERED THE PREVIOUS GAME IN THE SERIES, SPACE DEMONS.

"Why not?" he questioned uneasily. "What do you think would happen? And how would they know anyway?"

"Who knows?" Andrew replied, moving the joystick. "Anyway, it doesn't apply to us. Both of us did play Space Demons, and we all mastered it together. But that's why I can't play it at home. Paul shouldn't play it, you see—but try and tell him that."

Ben was peering at the screen. The sight of the cliff top aroused alarming memories that he was trying hard to forget. His feeling of unease deepened when the tiny figure appeared and jumped into the Skymaze.

"Andrew," he whispered, "that looks just like you!"

"I know!" Andrew replied. "It makes it seem so much more real. Clever, aren't I?" he added with pride, as his tiny screen self swung nimbly up a rope and on to the next screen.

"You have a go," he suggested to Ben when the game was over. The two boys changed places. As Ben took the joystick and brought the figure up on to the screen, he gave an inarticulate cry of surprise, and

29

Andrew exclaimed, "It's you!"

Ben dropped the joystick as though it was red hot. "That is creepy!" he said.

"It's not creepy," Andrew replied. "It's brilliant! Isn't it fun? You can really imagine it is you in the game. Go on, have a go. Nothing bad happens, I promise you."

As Ben nervously picked up the joystick again, Andrew added, "Anyway, you did say Space Demons was all my imagination. So what have you got to be scared about?"

"Nothing, I suppose," Ben conceded as he jumped himself into the Skymaze.

It seemed that Andrew was right. Ben finished his turn, and then Andrew played again, and then they took it in turns for the next hour, and apart from seeing their own images in the game they encountered nothing sinister.

Although they explored screen after screen, they did not come to the end of the Skymaze. Their highest score was 76, and Ben was drawing up a map, when Andrew had a brilliant idea.

"Plug the second joystick in," he suggested. "Let's see if we can play together."

They could. They could each take one path, and the screen split in half so they could each follow separate ways. Occasionally they met, and then the screen became single again. With two people playing, the score rose more swiftly, and because they learned from each other's mistakes, they found they could get through places that had seemed impassable before.

Ben broke the tense silence to make a comment. "One thing about this game is that you're unarmed. You can't defend yourself. You can only dodge."

"Yeah, I'd thought about that," Andrew said, dodging what looked like a waterfall. He knew from past experience that it was poisonous. "Perhaps that comes in a later stage. But it's a different sort of game from Space Demons, isn't it? It's got more of a sense of fun about it. You can't imagine it ever getting too lethal."

"I wish there was something that gave you more time, though," Ben said with a groan of frustration as the time ran out.

They started again. They were getting the timing of the early screens down to the split second now, moving and evading faster and faster, and climbing higher and higher. Eventually they met on a single screen where they had never been before. It was like a grotto in a mountain, with stalactites and stalagmites, and it looked so icy and remote and mysterious that both boys shivered involuntarily. The score stood at 123.

Then they almost jumped out of their skins as the computer spoke to them. It was not the voice they had heard in Space Demons, and which had haunted their dreams ever since; it sounded lighter, more neutral, and it gave no threats, only information.

This is the resource centre, it said. *Here you may choose one object to help you through the Skymaze. At this moment the choices are three: unlimited time, the gift of flight, and the power to defend yourself by force. Choose wisely. The Skymaze will respond to your choice.*

Andrew stole a quick look at Ben. His face was pale and he was frowning. But he still moved his figure forward.

The screen altered. Now they were more deeply inside the grotto. In front of them, hanging from the stalagmites, were three objects: a watch, a pair of winged boots, and a black cylindrical object that they both recognised immediately as the gun from the Space Demons game.

Andrew laughed in relief. "That's easy! We can handle that! Don't you see, it's a sort of test? We know you have to give up the gun to get out of Space Demons. There's no way we'd pick it up again!"

"I don't like it," Ben muttered. "Suppose the other objects do something weird that we don't know about? Suppose it's some kind of trick?"

"Oh, come on," Andrew begged him. "Let's go on with it. We can't stop now. You said you wanted more time—you take the watch and I'll take the boots."

"Okay, okay," Ben said. He moved the joystick. "But if it all goes wrong, Andrew, I'll never forgive you!"

His figure took the watch. Andrew's took the boots. There was a kind of pause in the game, a hush, into which the computer spoke gently, almost apologetically.

You have now activated the Skymaze.

"Oh migosh," Ben groaned. "What on earth do you think that means?"

"Only one way to find out!" Andrew laughed, and moved the joystick to play on.

But there was no response from the screen. Instead the images slowly faded, and over the original scene of cliff and stars ran a message.

STATE OF PLAY: LEVEL 2. SKYMAZE ACTIVATED. CONTROL PLAY IMPOSSIBLE.

No matter what they did, they could not get the program to run again.

CHAPTER THREE

On the same Saturday morning Elaine Taylor was sitting nervously on the floor in Studio A of the Contemporary Movement Group, watching a rehearsal and biting her knuckles as she always did when she was apprehensive. Her emotions were going up and down like an elevator: one moment she was wondering what on earth she was doing there, and if it would be all right to run away; and the next she was caught up in watching the class, half envious of the dancers, and half excited because of an inner, secret conviction that she was really one of them.

She might have run away if it had not been for the fact that her friend Linda Schulz was sitting next to her. Elaine had persuaded Linda with great difficulty to come with her. They were supposed to be doing some shopping—that was what Elaine had told her foster mother, Mrs Fields; and they had done some shopping, at least Linda had, so it wasn't totally untrue—but the real reason Elaine had come into the city that Saturday morning was to see Shaz Christie.

Shaz Christie herself was taking the dance class. She was so thin she looked two-dimensional, and so flexible she seemed liquid rather than solid, except that there was a taut, whippy strength about her. She looked like someone from the future, Elaine thought, with her thick black hair that stood straight up from her huge bony forehead and was streaked with glittering silver over each ear. The silver was echoed by a glistening stud in her nose. She was quite tall, as tall as some of the men in the class, and she radiated a kind of ferocious energy that Elaine found both attractive and alarming.

Elaine knew, from talking to her on the phone, that her voice was energetic too, and abrupt, as though she had no time to waste. Everything she did was quick and sudden. Elaine had nervously started to explain that she had heard that Shaz was looking for young people with circus skills to work on a new production with her, but Shaz had interrupted her.

"Be at the studio on Saturday morning at eleven. I'll have a look at what you can do."

Before Elaine had had time to say any more, Shaz had hung up, and Elaine was left in the phone box outside the school, holding the receiver and feeling like an idiot.

"Huh!" she had thought. "I'll show her!"

Now the time had come, she was not so confident. However, it was too late to escape now. The rehearsal came to an end, and the dancers drifted away. Elaine liked the way they looked, with their outlandish rehearsal gear of old sweat pants, bright leg-warmers and skinny tops. Most of them, men and women, had their hair cut very short, spiked and gelled. Two of them had orange hair, and one green. She ran her hand over her own red hair—she was glad she had had it cut. It was as short and spiky as the dancers'.

No one took any notice of the two girls, and Shaz would have walked out along with everyone else if

Linda had not given Elaine a dig in the ribs.

"Go on!" she hissed at her. "Go and grab her before she disappears."

Elaine jumped hastily to her feet and ran after the group.

"Hey," she said. "I mean, excuse me, Shaz?"

Shaz turned and looked coolly at her. There was a tiny butterfly tattooed in blue on the brown skin of her shoulder. Her look fired Elaine up again.

"I'm Elaine Taylor. I spoke to you on the phone." Her voice came out rather strongly, as though some of Shaz's energy had transferred itself to her.

"Oh, sure," Shaz said. "You want me to see you, don't you? Catch you later," she called to the dancers. Then she spoke again to Elaine. "What do you want to do? You want some music?"

"I brought a tape," Elaine said. "I've just put together a bit of a routine—some dance and some tumbling."

"Okay," Shaz said in her forceful, incisive voice. "I'll start it for you. You get in the centre of the floor."

Elaine took off her shoes and socks and then her jeans and sweatshirt. Underneath she was wearing a black leotard. She walked into the middle of the studio. Now that the moment had actually arrived, she was no longer nervous. The floor was black and shiny, and it felt good under her feet. She could see herself reflected in the floor-length mirrors and she looked at herself dispassionately, a tiny figure, all arms and legs and red hair. Then the music started and she began to dance.

Para bailar La Bamba
Para bailar La Bamba,
Se necesita una poca de gracia . . .

35

She had never had so much space to move in, and she put everything she had into the routine. She had a strict sequence of movements, but what she did instinctively, hardly aware that she was doing it, was flesh them out with emotion, so that she put into the routine all the things that were going on in her life at the moment. She danced her father coming and going, and the way she missed him and the free-and-easy life she used to have with him. She danced the discipline of gymnastics, the necessity of constant practice and improvement, and that led into the difficulty of living in someone else's house. She danced the ambivalence of her feelings for Jan and Les Fields, her foster parents; the gratitude and affection she felt for them; and the irritation and frustration of having to obey their rules.

Ba Ba Bamba, the music cried, *Ba Ba Bamba*.

She put into the routine her own rebelliousness, and that reminded her of Mario, so she added to it the way she felt about him, a feeling of having tamed a jungle animal, a mixture of pride, responsibility and fear. Then she ran out of feelings, so she just let the music take her, and she followed it with her whole being until, running out of breath, she did a series of back flips across the room and came to a halt in front of her audience of two.

Linda burst into spontaneous applause. Shaz said nothing at all for a moment, her face concentrating and expressionless. Then she smiled for the first time, bringing a wicked gleam into her eyes.

"You're not bad," she said. "Where'd you learn that stuff?"

"Dad and I travelled with a circus in New South Wales," Elaine said, feeling the old pang at the memories it brought back. She named some of the people she had known and Shaz nodded in recognition.

36

"I know them. You ready to work your butt off?"

"I suppose," Elaine said.

"It's not glamour, you know. It's bloody hard work." Shaz grinned her wicked grin again.

"I can hack it," Elaine said stubbornly.

"If you can't, you'll be out, it's as simple as that. You've got to turn up for every rehearsal unless you're actually in hospital."

"Sure."

"I'm starting rehearsing once a week for the next month. After that we'll be working two or three evenings a week, and possibly Saturdays too. Do you think you've got the time for that?"

"I'll make the time," Elaine promised.

"I'm trying to get a grant together, so there's a possibility I might be able to pay you something. And I'll need to have some kind of consent from your parents. Give me your phone number and I'll give them a ring tonight or tomorrow."

"This is my foster family," Elaine explained, writing the Fields' number down in Shaz's battered notebook.

"Oh, tough," Shaz said with a flicker of interest. "I know all about foster families! You making out all right?"

"On and off."

"You're probably doing better than I did, then!"

Elaine was fascinated, and longed to hear more, but Shaz shoved the notebook back in her bag. "I've got to dash. I'll see you here on Friday, six o'clock. Be late and you're dead."

She had gone out of the studio, and Elaine was putting on her shoes, when Shaz's voice called back to her through the open doors. "You got any boyfriends who do this sort of thing? I could use another couple of boys."

"I might know one," Elaine said, thinking of Ben.

"Bring him on Friday then. See ya!" The thin figure in the doorway waved and disappeared.

Linda's eyes were wide with amazement as they walked to the bus stop. "You're not really going to do it, are you, Elly?"

"You bet I am!" Elaine replied, alight with excitement. "Why the heck shouldn't I?"

"Do you think Mrs Fields will let you? My mum wouldn't."

"Why on earth not?"

"She looked a bit rough," Linda said dubiously. "You know, a bit like a punk."

"I think she looks great! I wish I looked like that." All the same, Linda's misgivings were undermining Elaine's elation. She remembered that she had not told the Fields anything about Shaz's planned production, which she herself had read about in the paper. She hadn't told them about her plans to telephone Shaz and get to meet her, and now that everything had worked out just as she had planned it, she realised she was going to have to do a lot of fast talking. "If only Dad was here," she thought painfully. Then she tried to reassure herself. "Of course they'll let me do it. It's the chance of a lifetime—they can't say no!"

Linda was distracted by the sight of a stunning outfit in a shop window, and by the time they got on the bus and sat down on the back seat, she was ready to talk about something else.

"What are you doing for the rest of the day?"

"Oh, I just remembered," Elaine said. The nerve-racking morning had put it out of her mind. "I'm going to the Show with John and Mario."

"Aw, lucky! Can I come with you?"

"I don't mind," Elaine said. "Will your mum let you?

Auntie Jan would probably be pleased if you came. She doesn't trust Mars—she always thinks he's going to land us in trouble. She doesn't know he's a reformed character. Well, sort of reformed," she added.

"Do you like him?" Linda loved talking about boys.

"I dunno," Elaine replied. She often asked herself the same question. "I don't think I do much at the moment."

"Do you fancy him, though?"

"No way!"

"But perhaps I do," Elaine thought privately. "Why else do I hang around with him all the time?"

"I think he's rather cute," Linda said with a giggle.

"Cute!" Elaine replied in amazement. "That's the last word I'd have used to describe him!"

"Well, you know what I mean!"

"What about Andrew Hayford? You used to think he was cute."

"Oh, I gave up on Andrew," Linda replied carelessly. "Anyway, since they've moved I never see him. I'm more into older guys now." She shot a teasing look at Elaine and said, "I thought Andrew rather liked you at one stage."

Elaine did not reply. She gazed out of the window and thought about the part Andrew Hayford had played in her life a year ago. In an unexpected way they had helped each other through a rough patch in their lives. She realised that her feelings for Andrew and Mario were rather similar; she felt as if they were all on the same side. "That must mean they're my friends," she decided. "And that's all they are!"

She turned back to Linda and said, "Well, I haven't got time for Mario or Andrew, gym keeps me too busy." Then she dug Linda in the ribs. "Did you hear that? I made a pun! Gym keeps me too busy, get it?"

"Very funny," Linda replied sarcastically. "I'd stick to the non-verbals if I was you!"

The two girls made plans to meet later, and, as Elaine had expected, Mrs Fields was quite relieved to hear that Linda was going with her to the Show.

"You'll keep an eye on Mario Ferrone, won't you, Linda?" she said, when Linda arrived to collect Elaine. "Don't let him do anything stupid. I know you're sensible!"

She was preparing to have a quiet afternoon with her knitting and the paper. She always read the Real Estate ads at the weekend and quite often she and Les would drive out to open inspections. They said they were looking for somewhere to live when they retired, but since that was still some time away for both of them, Elaine knew it was mainly because they enjoyed looking inside other people's houses. They liked it when Elaine went with them, and sometimes she liked it too—it *was* endlessly fascinating to see how other people lived, especially rich people—but she would much prefer to go to the Show with her friends. She just wished the Fields wouldn't spend the evening worrying about her, as she suspected they would.

"What about me?" she said indignantly, "Don't you think I'm sensible?"

"You forget you're only thirteen—you act like you know it all. And I sometimes think you egg those boys on!"

"I do not!" But Elaine knew there was a little bit of truth in it. She liked it when people took risks and did things they weren't supposed to do. It made life more exciting. "I never used to be like that when I lived with Dad," she thought, "but life usually was pretty exciting then. Always on the move, and never knowing what was going to happen next. It's all very well living in a proper home and being looked after, but it needs a bit of livening up sometimes."

"And come back as soon as the fireworks are finished."

"We will, we will," Elaine sighed.

"Don't worry, Mrs Fields, my dad's going to meet us after and bring us home," Linda said, giving Elaine a dig in the ribs to get her to shut up. "And I'll make sure everyone behaves themselves."

"Like hell you will," Elaine said when they were out in the street. "Everyone thinks you're so well behaved all the time. How do you do it?"

"I've just got that sort of face," Linda replied. "Useful, isn't it?" She took out a mirror and some lipstick from her bag, and coloured her lips pink. Then she put mascara on her eyelashes. "How's that look?" She fluttered her eyelashes at Elaine.

"Looks okay."

"You want some?"

"You think I could do my eyes like Shaz Christie?"

"What is this, hero worship?" Linda muttered sarcastically, but she took out her eyebrow pencil. "Hold still!"

Elaine stood stock-still, keeping her eyes wide open while Linda outlined them with pencil and darkened her lashes with mascara.

"Gee, that looks gross!" she groaned when she looked at herself in the mirror. Her eyes looked enormous, like those of a waif on a greetings card. "I look like someone socked me in the eye!"

"Well, you can't take it off now," Linda replied. "I think it makes you look sort of interesting! Now all you need is the nose stud and the tattoo."

"Yeah, a little butterfly on the shoulder," Elaine

41

said. "Don't tempt me. I've got to try and look like a sensible person, otherwise Auntie Jan's going to renege!"

"Did you ask her about Shaz?" Linda demanded excitedly. "What did she say?"

"She didn't say no. She said she'd think about it." Elaine crossed her fingers and waved them in Linda's face. "I'd cross my ears if I could." She wiggled them instead. "But I've got a feeling it's going to be okay!"

Linda put the make-up away, then twisted her hair up into a snazzy ponytail on the top of her head. She had managed to transform herself completely from the quiet-looking, well-behaved young girl who had so impressed Mrs Fields. She gave Elaine a wink. "Right!" she said. "Let's go and have fun!"

When they met the boys at the bus stop, Mario was scowling and John had his worried look.

"What's up with you two?" Elaine said.

"Don't worry about it," Mario answered angrily. "It's not worth wasting time on." The bus arrived and he jumped on it and swung his way down to the back on the seat bars.

"What happened?" Elaine asked John as they paid the fares.

"Just another bust-up at home," he replied philosophically. "You'd think Dad and Mars would know how to get on with each other by now, wouldn't you? After all, they have lived in the same house for fourteen years! Dad can't seem to get it into his head that if he forbids Mars to do something it's just like telling him he's got to do it."

"What did he forbid?" Linda said eagerly.

"Going to the Show today. Mum had promised we could, and she said she'd give us some money to spend,

42

and when Dad heard about it he hit the roof. He said we hadn't got the money to waste on things like that, and we'd only get into trouble there, and we weren't to go."

Linda's eyes widened in excitement. "Then how come you're going?"

"We just ran away before he could stop us," John said. "Well, Mario ran away, and I followed him. But I don't know what's going to happen when we get back," he added with some concern.

"Sounds like a promising start!" Linda said, shooting an admiring look at Mario from under her spiky lashes. He ignored her, scowling out of the window.

Mario remained unmoved by any of Linda's approaches, and when they got to the showground he did his best to lose her and John. He finally achieved this when Linda was distracted by the huge task of choosing show bags.

"Come on!" he hissed in Elaine's ear, grabbing her by the arm and hustling her away from the show bag counter. "Let's go on some rides."

"No, wait," she said. "I don't want to lose the others."

"I do!" he replied with a grin. "We'll meet up with them after. It's more fun with just the two of us. I can't stand that Linda. She loves herself!"

"She doesn't really," Elaine replied. "It's just her style. She's okay when you get to know her."

"Well, my plans for life don't include that!" Mario returned. He pulled her through the crowd of people all fighting their way towards the counters, and out through the exit. Outside it was nearly dark. The air was damp and cold, and smelt of animals and hot chips.

Elaine looked at Mario and said wickedly, "Anyway, she thinks you're cute."

"Cute!" Mario snorted in disgust. "Nobody thinks I'm cute!" He let go of Elaine's arm and draped his own across her shoulders, pulling her in close to him, so that for a moment she was acutely conscious of his thin, spare body. She ducked away. "Let go! You don't have to maul me."

"I'm not mauling you, you idiot, I'm just being friendly! Nobody in their right mind would want to maul you anyway. You've got nothing to maul!"

"Huh!" Elaine felt highly insulted. "You can go on by yourself. I'm going back to find the others."

"No, don't," he said with a flashing grin. "Come on, I'm sorry. I'll win you one of those big toys. You want one?"

"Don't you think I could win myself one if I wanted one?"

"I think you could do anything you wanted, but I want to win one for you." Mario's voice was unusually nice, and Elaine looked at him suspiciously. She hoped very much he was not getting sentimental. She had the idea it would make life very complicated. When she was feeling sensible she swore to herself she would have nothing to do with him, but she didn't feel sensible very often lately, and the one thing about Mario was, he was not boring. There was always the possibility of life getting dangerous when he was around, and she found this irresistible.

"Let's have a match," she said. "I bet I can beat you!"

"What's the bet?"

"Whatever you like."

"Loser has to stand up on the Mad Mouse?"

44

"You tired of life or something?"

"I'm not going to lose," he pointed out.

"Okay," Elaine said coolly, determined not to back down now. She gestured towards the nearest shooting stand. "You go first."

Mario's first two shots missed the little ducks, but after that he hit every one down. After several goes he won a huge panda.

"Your shot," he said, handing the rifle to Elaine. She picked it up and squinted through it. She was sure she was aiming straight at the ducks, but she missed the first three, hit four, then missed two. She didn't win anything.

"Bad luck," Mario said. He gave her the panda. "Here you are. Consolation prize. The sights were wrong," he went on as they walked away. "You had to compensate."

"You might have told me before!"

"No way! We were having a bet!"

"You'd do anything to win, wouldn't you?" she said bitterly.

"That's life!" he replied. "If you can't take it, don't play it. Now, which way to the Mad Mouse?"

"It can't be that difficult," Elaine thought. "I know I can balance, and if there's a long enough straight stretch, I can just jump up quickly and get down again before the turn." But when they approached the roller coaster it looked alarmingly high, much higher than she had remembered.

"Want to back down?" Mario said teasingly.

"Of course not!"

"I'll give you an alternative." They were waiting in line for the tickets, and he whispered in her ear, "Give me a kiss and I'll let you off!"

Elaine pushed him away. "I'd rather die!"

She nearly did. She took her chance on the first stretch in case it was the only one, shoved the panda at Mario, crouched on the seat, straightened up, let go, saw the whole showground spread out beneath her for one dizzying moment, and then felt the car shift as the turn came up, far faster than she had expected. She threw herself down, but as the car whipped around the turn, the reflex flung her in the opposite direction, and her body slewed across the back. Mario grabbed her from behind. For a second it seemed that they must both fly out of the car together, and then the track swung the other way and threw them back in again. Only the panda fell.

They clung to each other and then scrabbled frantically to get a grip on the handrail before the next downward plunge. Elaine's heart was stammering and for a moment she thought she was going to throw up, but then an incredible feeling of elation took hold of her, and she started to laugh.

Mario looked sideways at her, his face white beneath the arc lights. "You okay?" He thought she was crying, but when he saw from her face that she was laughing, he grinned wildly back at her and gripped her shoulder harder.

When the ride came to an end they staggered off together, still holding on to each other, and came face to face with a furious security guard holding the panda.

"You try that again, you dumb kids, and you'll be slung out! You nearly got yourselves killed!"

"We didn't do anything wrong," Mario said innocently. "She wanted to get off, and I had to stop her. Can we have our panda back?"

Adults always reacted badly to Mario and the guard was no exception. His face tightened in anger as he leaned over. He was so close to them Elaine could smell onions on his breath.

"Watch your step, kid," he warned. "I'll be happy to escort you out of here."

Mario started to say something rude, but Elaine interrupted quickly. "Shut up, Mars." Then she said to the guard, "Give us back the panda. Please."

Grudgingly the guard held it out to her. She grabbed it and they ducked away through the crowd. When they were some way from the Mad Mouse, they slowed to a walk.

"Did anyone ever tell you you were crazy?" Mario said admiringly to Elaine.

"I think I must be," she replied. She was wondering why on earth she had done it. She had so much going for her at the moment, so much that should make her hang on to life, but at that split second on the Mad Mouse nothing had mattered. Nothing had been important, except to stand up. And she had done it, and now she felt terrific.

"I'm starving," she said.

They stopped to get hot dogs and Cokes, and while they were eating them and watching the crowd, Elaine caught sight of a face she recognised immediately, even though it was some months since she had last seen it. She nudged Mario, making him choke on his drink.

"Look, there's Andrew Hayford."

Mario screwed up his hot dog wrapper violently, and threw it on the ground. Then he turned to look at Andrew. He had not seen him for a long time either, but he had thought about him a lot, and even dreamed about him disturbingly. There was some mysterious bond between them, doubly strong because last year, when they were playing Space Demons, Andrew had tried to destroy him and had then come back to save his life. Mario felt a sweep of some extremely powerful emotion that he could not put a name to: it was neither hate nor love, but a disconcerting mixture of the two. The emotion was stirred up more by Andrew's self-confident manner, the dazzling smile on his undeniably good-looking face, and the way he raced up to Mario and Elaine as though he was certain they would be delighted to see him.

In a way they were. People usually were pleased to see Andrew, in spite of themselves; and even after they had decided firmly they did not like him, there was still something about him that attracted them.

"What are you guys doing here?" he demanded.

"What do you think?" Mario replied, on edge. "You don't own this place too, you know."

"Be better if I did," Andrew said, surveying the scene with distaste. "It wouldn't be so boring if I ran it. All this stuff is so weak. Same old thing year after year. I don't know why people keep coming to it."

"Can't think of anything better to do, I suppose," Elaine said. "Same as you."

"I just came to keep Ben company," Andrew replied. "But I've lost him."

"That reminds me," Elaine said. "We've lost John and Linda too. Perhaps we'd better start looking for them."

"No hurry," Mario told her, taking her hand possessively.

For some reason the gesture annoyed Andrew. He tried not to stare at their hands. "Where'd you get the panda?"

"Mars won it shooting ducks," Elaine said, and the memory of the bet and its consequence made her laugh again. Her eyes lit up with excitement. "The Show's okay," she told Andrew. "You just have to be crazy and liven things up a bit."

"But Andrew's not the crazy type," Mario said. "He's a nice straight college boy now."

"Not altogether," Andrew said defensively. He was also feeling some strong and unfamiliar emotions. When he had first met Mario Ferrone, he had loathed him instinctively. Then he had come to understand him a little, to admire him a lot, and even to want to like him. But liking someone so different from himself was not easy. He and Mario had done a few things together a year ago, but then they had drifted apart. Their backgrounds and their values were too different for them to have much in common. Now Andrew realised that what was making him uncomfortable was the feeling that Elaine and Mario were a unit, a couple, and that they were on one side of the fence and he was on the other. He almost envied them. He wanted to say something that would impress them. He wanted to remind them that once the three of them had faced each other with their defences down. Once, briefly, they had all been on the same side.

"I got a new game last week," he remarked to Mario.

Elaine felt Mario's whole body shudder, as though Andrew had touched an open nerve, but he replied casually, "Yeah? What's it like?"

"It's cool fun. You can come and play it some time. It's called . . ."

But Mario and Elaine did not hear what it was called, for at that moment Mario spotted Linda through the crowd and he started running. Since he was still holding Elaine's hand, she had to run too. Andrew did not want to lose sight of them just yet. He chased after them.

"Hey!" Elaine exclaimed, as Mario pushed rudely

through a bunch of people who were dropping balls in clowns' mouths. "What's up? What's the hurry? Oh, sorry," she added, as she stepped on someone's toes and stumbled. "Hang on, Mars!" she shrieked. "I've dropped my panda!"

As they paused to scoop up the fluffy toy, Elaine glanced up at the face belonging to the person whose toes had got in the way.

"Oh, sorry!" she said again, and then, "Oh, help!"

There was an angry yell. "You two again! That's it! That's your last chance! I'm chucking you out."

The three began to run in earnest, for the person over whom Elaine had stumbled, and who was now after them with a determined look on his face, was the same security guard who had warned them beside the Mad Mouse.

They struggled through the ranks of people, pushing and shoving and leaving a trail of anger and swearing in their wake, until they came to the end of the sideshows and were running towards the back of the showground, with the rides on their right and the pavilions and arenas on their left. Mario had let go of Elaine's hand and was trying to outstrip Andrew. They were both some way ahead of her. Elaine slowed down a little, and took a quick look over her shoulder. She could see the guard far behind them in the distance, looking curiously diminished, as though he was shrinking. Something was happening to her perception that made her giddy as if with vertigo, and something had happened to the world around her.

"It's too dark," she thought rapidly to herself, as a sudden twinge of terror gripped her. Everywhere was too dark. Too dark and too quiet. She looked behind her again. She could see, very far away, the bright lights and crowds of the sideshows, as though she was looking down a long dark tunnel.

"Why isn't there anyone else here?" she called in panic to the boys. "What's happening?" Looking up, she realised she could see the stars far more clearly than she should have been able to. They hung like huge lamps, almost close enough to touch, no longer dimmed by the harsh lights of the Show.

Mario and Andrew stood motionless ahead of her. As Elaine ran towards them, Mario stepped forward. She could tell by the way he moved that he wasn't afraid at all, even though he was quivering. "What's happening, Andy?" he said.

"I don't know," Andrew replied, and he didn't sound at all scared either. "But we've been here before. Don't you remember?"

Of course they remembered. For the last year they had been there in dreams, and had relived the terror, the excitement and the promise. The stars were the stars from the final stage of Space Demons, and beneath their feet the cliff top was solidifying.

CHAPTER FOUR

It was like being in another world, in a different dimension. Behind them were the lights of the Show, tiny but quite bright and distinct in the distance. In front of them something was taking shape in the sky, as though it was being poured out and freezing solid as it fell. It spiralled away in every direction, faint and shimmery but unmistakably there.

Mario drew his breath in sharply, but he did not speak. He was too busy staring at the scene before them. Andrew said, unable to disguise the excitement in his voice, "It's the Skymaze! It's the game! It's . . . it's come alive!"

With a shudder Mario came alive too. "What are we waiting for?" he demanded. "Let's go in!"

"Hang on," said Elaine. "Don't rush things. Are you sure it's safe, Andrew? What's going to happen?"

"It's quite safe," Andrew assured them. "It's just a fun game, not a shoot-'em-up. There's nothing trying to get you—you just have to be careful not to touch some things. But I know what they all are, I'll tell you about them. Oh, and you have to be careful not to fall too far. That kills you."

"Great!" Elaine replied. "Does it kill you once and

for all, or just in the game?"

"That's what we'll have to find out."

"You're joking!"

"It's okay, you get three lives."

"That's two more than you had on the Mad Mouse," Mario reminded her. Then he added, "I didn't think you were scared of anything."

"You can wait here if you *are* scared," Andrew told her patronisingly.

That did it. Scared or not, there was no way Elaine was going to be left behind while the boys went on together. "How do you get in?" she demanded, squinting upwards at the sky.

"You have to jump on to one of the strands—can you see them?" When the others nodded, Andrew went on, "We'll take the one on the left first, it's the easiest, and if you miss it you don't lose a life, you just fall back on to the cliff. You go first, Mars, then Elly, and I'll go last. That way no one will be stuck on their own. And wait for me once you're in the maze. We must stay together."

Mario nodded. He located the strand and leaped upwards. They saw him grasp on to *something*, they saw the *something* wrinkle and stretch, as though a hole was appearing in the sky itself, and then Mario disappeared and the sky closed over again.

"Oh migosh!" Elaine breathed. "Where's he gone to?"

"Now you," Andrew ordered.

She hesitated. "What am I going to do with the panda?"

"Leave it down here. We'll pick it up again when we get out." He took it from her. "See you up there," he added cheerfully as she steadied herself for the jump.

As she leaped, Elaine had a moment of panic that

53

she had missed the strand, but then she felt it thicken under her fingers. It was like a steel cable, thick but flexible, swaying slightly in the space wind. Elaine pulled herself upwards, felt the sky open around her, and felt the ground, if that was what you could call it, solidify under her hands and elbows. She wriggled through and stood up.

She was alone in a small, cold, silvery space. A silver ladder led upwards into the clouds, and something like a rope bridge, also silver, went away to the right, though she could not see how far it went or what it led to. There was no sign of Mario.

"Where the hell has he gone to?" Andrew said when he came wriggling through the wrinkle in the sky. "He should have stayed here. If he's gone on alone he could be anywhere."

"I thought you said it was quite safe," Elaine accused him.

"I thought it would be safe. It *is* safe if you're sensible."

"It's no use expecting Mario to be sensible," Elaine exclaimed angrily.

"Well, don't get excited about it," Andrew replied. "We'll just go and look for him. He probably went on ahead."

"What if he's fallen? What if he touched one of those things you said we shouldn't?"

"We have to find out sooner or later what happens if we do those things," Andrew pointed out. "Which do you fancy, the ladder or the bridge?"

"You're the expert! Which one gets us out of here? And what have you got on your feet? You weren't wearing those before!"

"They're my flying boots! I chose them last time I played the game. Isn't it fantastic!"

"Groovy!" Elaine agreed sarcastically. "So which is the way out?"

"We don't want to get out! We want to go on! Let's try the ladder; the bridge is fun, but there's a tricky bit when you get off it. You mustn't step on the flowers. Go on, you go first!"

"Lucky I'm not afraid of heights, isn't it," Elaine grumbled as she began to climb.

As they went on from level to level, however, she realised she was enjoying herself. Sometimes it was like flying, as they swung across bottomless chasms; sometimes it was like sliding, as they zoomed down long tunnels; sometimes it was as demanding as any gymnastics she had ever done, and she needed all her skill and balance to continue. She realised too that although Andrew had the advantage of having played the game before, and, because he wore the winged boots, had no fear of falling, her training had made her as skilful as he was, and she got out of trouble as quickly as he did.

As they climbed further and further, there was still no sign of Mario, and even Andrew began to look anxious. He checked his watch. "I wonder what happens when the time runs out," he said. "I wish Ben was here, he chose unlimited time, then we could stay in forever."

"Forever might be a bit too long," Elaine commented as she leaped from point to point across to where Andrew was standing. He put out an arm to steady her. "Look out," he said. "Some things are likely to fall on your head here, and if they touch you, you're dead!"

Elaine looked up nervously, and then jumped lightly to one side. A glowing light fell noiselessly past her. "Eeek," she said. "Creepy!"

55

Then she jumped again, in the other direction, but Andrew was jumping that way too, and they knocked into each other. Andrew slipped and half fell; the boots kept him from falling downwards, but he could not avoid the light. It brushed against his shoulder. Elaine saw his face go white. He gave her a half wave—and disappeared.

"Andrew!" she shrieked.

She was on her own.

"What the hell do I do now," she thought angrily. Another light came noiselessly down, and she jumped backwards in alarm. The leap took her back on to one of the stepping points. For a moment she wobbled and nearly fell, then she regained her balance and leaped for the next point.

"I'm getting out of here!" she said aloud. She began to retrack down the Skymaze.

It was much harder going down than up, and it was harder alone than with someone else. Finally, however, Elaine came to the top of a silver ladder that she was sure was the first one she had climbed. She began to descend it. By now she had become almost used to the background noises and sound effects of the Skymaze, and so she was surprised and rather alarmed to hear a curious noise from below, one she had not heard before. It was a sort of scrabbling and rustling. Then the ladder began to sway. She stopped climbing down and clung on, listening intently. Someone—or something—was climbing up from below.

She was wondering whether to start scrambling up again or to keep going down, when the person (or *thing*) came close enough for her to hear its breathing. Suddenly it grabbed her ankle.

"Elly!" it said. "Get out of the way!"

56

"Mars!" she said in relief. "What happened to you?"

"I got killed a couple of times and had to start again. First time I stepped on some deadly flowers, and then I fell off the tightrope. Where's Andrew?"

"He got zapped by a light and left me on my own."

"Aw, diddums! He'll be okay, he's probably coming up again now. Come on, hurry up and get out of the way. I can't wait to get up there again."

"I'm going down! *You* get out of *my* way!"

"What're you going down for? The aim of the game is to get to the end. You can't chicken out!"

"I am not chickening out!"

"Then go on up, or I'll shake you off!" Mario let go of her ankle and began to swing on the ladder, making it sway back and forth alarmingly. Elaine clung on harder. "Stop it, you bully," she yelled. The ladder was swinging wildly now, making long sweeps from side to side. Mario reached up, grabbed Elaine again, and began to pull on her leg. "Go up or I'll pull you off!" he threatened.

"You'd better be careful," she warned him. "You've only got one life left. If you fall now, you've had it!"

"So stop being so stubborn and let me up!"

"You let me down!"

Mario was starting to swear at her when he was silenced by a brilliant flash of light. For a moment Elaine saw their tiny figures silhouetted on the swaying ladder, then the whole scene began to recede rapidly from her point of vision. Briefly she felt herself in two places at once. Then her real self became more real and more solid, and the tiny image disappeared completely.

She was standing with Mario and Andrew back on the edge of the showground. The fireworks had started; there was a boom behind them and another flash of light as patterns flowered in the sky. The lights and the noise of the Show came rushing back all around them, making them reel and close their eyes. When they opened them again, the stars and the cliff top were gone.

Mario gave Andrew a punch on the shoulder, grinning at him in delight. "That was okay, wasn't it?"

"So far, so good!" Andrew replied. He was trembling with excitement. "What happened to you?"

"I just went to see what was round the corner, over the bridge, and the flowers got me. I sort of blacked out and found myself on the cliff again, so I jumped into the maze and came after you, but then I fell off something else."

"You should have waited for us. That's what I told you!"

Mario shrugged. "Oh well, no harm done. At least we found out what happens if you lose a life."

"You didn't find out what happens if you lose three," Elaine pointed out rather sourly.

Andrew peered at her. "What's the matter with you?"

She turned away from them. The last of the fireworks were fading from the sky, and a few spots of rain were beginning to fall. The panda lay on the ground, its fur dusty and stained. Elaine picked it up. She suddenly felt unaccountably lonely and depressed. "Come on," she said. "We must meet up with the others. They'll be wondering where on earth we are."

"Didn't you like it, though?" Andrew was hurrying alongside her, trying to keep up with her as she walked briskly towards the gate where they had arranged to meet Linda's father. "Didn't you think it was great?"

"I didn't think it was great being pulled off the

ladder," she snapped back at him, loud enough for Mario to hear. Mario took no notice, but sauntered along, whistling through his teeth and looking pleased with himself. Elaine was growing more and more irritated. "You're a bully!" she said to him. "You never think of anyone but yourself. You would have chucked me off that ladder, wouldn't you?"

"You should've got out of the way," Mario replied. "It's a game, you've got to play it all out or it's not worth playing. I thought you had more guts. What happened then, anyway, Andy? Why did it stop then?"

"You were cheating," Elaine said. "That's what made it stop."

"Get away! That had nothing to do with it. Anyway, I wasn't cheating!"

"I think the time ran out." Andrew interrupted what was about to become a brawl. "We should have had Ben with us, he's the one with unlimited time."

"How d'you mean?"

"When Ben and I played the game on the computer, we had a choice of objects to help us through the Skymaze. Ben chose a watch—unlimited time—and I chose some winged boots. Back there . . ." Andrew gestured behind them, still hardly able to put what had happened into words, "I was wearing the boots." He was silent for a moment, and then went on in a voice quiet with amazement, "I could fly!"

"Hah!" Mario shouted in excitement. "No kidding! This is fantastic!" Unable to contain his feelings, he leaped up in the air and yelled. When he came down again, oblivious to the stares he was getting from the people around them, he said to Andrew, trying to keep his voice down, "So . . . so . . . so if we all play it, we get more things to help us?"

"That's what I reckon," Andrew replied.

"And then when it . . . it comes to life, we have them to use for real?"

Andrew's face was split in half by his enormous grin. "Yeah!"

"Listen, my man, we'd better get together and play that game."

"Just what I think," Andrew agreed. "What about you, Elly? Are you in?"

"No way!"

"Aw, go on," Andrew pleaded. "It won't be the same without you. You were marvellous back there."

"She's scared," Mario said scornfully.

"Is that all you can say?" Elaine replied angrily. "You sound like a parrot, saying the same thing over and over again. Can't you get it into your thick skull that I can choose what I want to do, and unlike you I don't base my choices on whether people think I'm a coward or not! I don't give a stuff what you think of me. And I've got other things to do with my time than play these dumb games with you."

"Are you mad at me?" Mario said with interest.

"You don't even rate being mad at!"

"She's mad at you," Andrew observed. The boys rolled their eyes upwards and laughed. Elaine was the one who felt on the outside now. She was relieved to see Linda and John waiting by the exit, and she walked quickly away from Andrew and Mario towards them. Behind her, the two boys made plans to meet again as soon as possible. Then they slapped palms, and Andrew went to look for Ben. He couldn't wait to tell him what had happened.

CHAPTER FIVE

"Did you tell him about last night?" It was Sunday morning and Mario was sitting in front of the computer in Ben Challis's house, gazing enthralled at the cliff top and the starry sky of the first screen of Skymaze.

"I tried to," Andrew replied, "but he wasn't very receptive, were you, Benny boy?"

"Don't call me that," Ben snapped. He was still annoyed with Andrew for disappearing at the Show. He had spent quite an unpleasant half hour looking for him, and he hadn't got to do half the things he'd wanted to. Then Andrew had turned up, not in the least repentant, just full of how he had met up with Mario and Elaine, and how the game had come alive, and they had played it for real. Ben didn't believe it. He didn't want to believe it. He didn't want to be playing the game now, but Mario had turned up, and he and Andrew had bullied him into letting them use the computer.

"Although," he thought despondently, "they didn't even really bully me. They just assumed they were going to play it and I let them. Why do I?" he wondered. "I let people do whatever they want to do, even though I don't think it's a good idea." The realisation depressed him.

Andrew and Mario took no notice of him at all.
Instead they settled down to play Skymaze. Rather
morosely, Ben watched them move through the early
stages of the game, noticing with a prickle of anxiety
how the second figure was now a tiny image of Mario.

"There are the freaky flowers!" Mario exclaimed. "I
know all about them!" He jumped his screen self
lightly over them. "This is ace, Andy! We can practise
on the game, and then when it comes up for real again,
we'll be experts and get through the whole thing."

"That's right." Andrew didn't mind at all being
called Andy by Mario. He wondered why he should
hate it so much from his stepfather. "And look, I've still
got my flying boots. Whatever you choose stays with
you, wherever the Skymaze is." He made his little
image leap off the ladder it was on and fly downwards,
his eyes sparkling as he recalled, in his own limbs, what
it had felt like the night before. "We're going to need
Ben again," he went on. "He chose unlimited time. We
definitely need that to get through the maze. I wonder
what happens when you do get through it, when you
get to the end? What's it leading to? Where's it going?"

"Only one way to find out!" Mario muttered
between his teeth.

"My sentiments entirely!" Andrew agreed.

They played without speaking, concentrating
furiously on getting through the maze. Finally they
came to the ice-white grotto. Into the silence of the
game the voice spoke once more:

*This is the resource centre. Here you may choose one
object to help you through the Skymaze. At this
moment the choices are two: the elixir of healing and the
power to defend yourself by force. Choose wisely. The
Skymaze will respond to your choice.*

"Sheesh!" Mario exclaimed. "I don't want the elixir of freaking healing. I'll take the gun!"

"Don't you ever learn anything?" Andrew said quickly. "It's the gun from Space Demons. You can't take that!"

Mario looked at it longingly, biting his lip, remembering the feeling of power it had once given him. He swore under his breath. "Stupid game! What a drag! Playing dumb tricks on us. You think you're so smart," he said angrily to the computer screen. "You think you can push us around. Well, we're going to fix you!"

He moved his figure forward to pick up the flask.

You have now activated the Skymaze, the computer informed him politely.

The game seemed to freeze for a few seconds, and the boys sat as if frozen too. A hiatus had occurred during which everyday reality went on hold, and when it started up again it was subtly but intrinsically altered. Nobody moved or said anything until, with a flicker, the original scene reappeared and across the screen ran the words: STATE OF PLAY: LEVEL 2: SKYMAZE ACTIVATED. CONTROL PLAY IMPOSSIBLE.

Ben shook his head sharply, and Andrew rubbed his eyes.

"Now what?" Mario exclaimed tensely, pushing back his chair and stretching his arms up over his head. "What do we do now? Do we go back to the showground? Do you think it's still there?" His eyes glittered as though he was feverish.

"I don't know." Andrew stood and stretched too. He was thinking hard. "It wouldn't have been at the Show if we hadn't been there," he said slowly. "I don't think we have to look for it. I think it finds us—I mean, it appears where we are."

"Anywhere?"

"We don't know that yet. It's only happened once."

"Let's go out somewhere," Ben said, looking rather nervously from Andrew to Mario and back again. He did not like the expression on their faces. They were hooked by the game, just as they had been by Space Demons, and they would stop at nothing until they had played it to the end. He wanted to get away from the computer, sitting there so innocently, yet filled with such potential danger. However, as soon as he had made the suggestion, he wished he hadn't. Mario flashed a wicked look at him.

"Good idea!" he said with feigned casualness. "Who knows, anything might happen!"

"You're right," Andrew said. Not knowing where they would encounter the Skymaze added to his excitement. It could happen at any moment! He realised he was shivering with anticipation. "Where shall we go?"

"Darren's taken his trail bike up to the quarry," Ben said. He had a most unfamiliar feeling of wanting to be with his older brother, as if Darren could protect him from Andrew and Mario. "He might give us a go on it." He remembered ruefully how, a few weeks earlier, he had run to Andrew's house to get away from Darren; now he was running from Andrew and Mario back to his brother. He felt like a pinball ricocheting out of control, bouncing from one to the other. And they had no more feeling for him than the buttons had for the ball.

"We'll come with you." Mario put his arm over Ben's shoulder as they went out through the door. "We want to stay very close to you!" It looked like a friendly gesture, but the grip on his arm gave Ben a moment's unpleasant insight into how it must feel to be a hostage.

Outside it was a soft and beautiful spring day, to which Andrew and Mario were completely oblivious. The three boys walked in silence up the road behind Ben's house, ducked under the fence at the end, and began to climb the hill that led to the quarry.

Ben knew the whole area like his own back yard. He had explored it from end to end ever since he was a little kid. As they followed the narrow path up from the creek bank where wild freesias and onion weed starred the brilliant green grass with white, and through the tangled olive bushes and young gum trees, he realised that he loved it; it soothed and comforted him to be out here among the trees, where birds swooped and called and where he could feel the warmth of the spring sun on his back. Above his head, clusters of leaves held high by gum trees rustled and quivered in the wind, all movement and life; and further above, white and grey clouds sailed across from the south-west, casting their shadows on the Hills face below and lightening and darkening the quarry so that it looked alternately purple and gold.

The quarry had been hacked out of the side of the hill when the city was first built, providing the beautiful bluestone for which it was famous. At that time rail tracks had run up the steep slope to bring the stone down to the railway. "Hundreds of people must have worked here," Ben thought. He tried to imagine them, dynamiting and cutting, men and machines going at full blast. Now the quarry was deserted except for birds, rabbits and foxes: a wilderness of fallen boulders and rocks, perfect for wild and dangerous games.

The quarry itself had been cut in a sort of irregular T shape, and the way in was up the narrow stroke of the T. It was like walking through a canyon. Just before the entrance, where the topsoil and gravel had been heaped long ago, a sort of natural bike track had evolved, with slopes and jumps that were greatly appreciated by the local BMXers and trail bike riders. As the three boys started to climb the last slope before the quarry, they could hear clearly the snarl of a trail bike.

"Isn't it illegal to ride those here?" Andrew said, out of breath as they struggled to the top.

"Yeah. Darren's meant to stick to the dirt road down by the railway, but the jumps are so good up here he can't resist them," Ben replied, gratified to notice that he was not out of breath at all. At least he was fitter than Andrew!

Mario was wheezing a bit too when they all stood on the grassy top of the first hill, the city spread out behind them, the quarry rising in front. "You'll have to give up smoking," Ben needled him. Now they were out of doors, away from the computer and the game, his confidence was returning. Out here he felt equal to Andrew and Mario: he felt as if he could take them both on. He felt the freedom the pinball must feel when it is between two buttons, rolling free on the table. The person in the helmet, bumping towards them on the trail bike, was his own brother, Darren. And if Darren let him have a go on the bike he'd be able to show the other boys a thing or two.

But when Darren lifted the helmet to speak to them, his face, streaked with dirt and sweat, was unwelcoming, and his blue eyes, bright with exertion, were unfriendly; when Ben said, "Give us a go," and took hold of the handle bars, Darren twisted them away from him. "Not today, little brother. You go and play cops and robbers with your buddies."

Booiinngg. Ben could literally feel the jolt as he

66

came up against his brother's hostility and began to spin away again.

"Aw, come on, Darren, you promised!" he protested, but he had already realised that his hope that his brother might protect him was absolutely futile. Darren ignored his plea, and would have taken off again if Mario had not given the back wheel a contemptuous kick and observed, "Weak bike!"

"You'd better watch it, Ferrone, I can make a lot of trouble for you!"

"Oh, big man!" Mario sneered. "What kind of trouble would that be?"

"Oh, great!" Ben thought. "Now they're going to get into a punch up." He wondered which side he would be on if that happened. Or if he could just disappear and be on no one's side. He had a moment's pleasing fantasy that the two of them would beat the hell out of each other—but then, they would almost certainly blame him for it afterwards and make him pay, no matter who won or lost.

"Come on," he said. "Let's go and climb up the quarry."

He and Andrew moved on ahead. Mario gave the bike one more kick, then jumped back as Darren revved it up and swung around to take the course again. The bike's snarl reverberated and echoed round the hillside, drowning out the sound of the birds. It struck Ben suddenly as intrusive and cruel. Darren, crouched low over it, in his black helmet and jacket, looked like an alien. He had been mad to expect protection from him.

The bike raced up the slope, rounded the curve, and leaped the first two mounds; and then Mario, who had been hidden behind an olive tree, jumped out in front of it with a wild yell.

Darren swerved to miss him, slid sideways, lost control, and landed in a heap in a prickle bush, the bike on top of him.

"Learn to ride!" Mario shouted derisively, and ran laughing after Ben and Andrew.

Darren picked himself up, swearing vilely. He got on the bike again, turned in a broad circle to get speed up, and began to chase after them.

"Run!" Mario shouted as he tore past Andrew. They were running up part of the bike track, and Darren was gaining on them alarmingly, but then the track turned to the left and the boys ran straight on, up a little path that followed the rim of the quarry. On their right the cliff dropped sheer to the boulder-strewn floor. On their left at first the gentler slope of the hill continued, but this gradually narrowed until they were on a thin track leading precariously between two cliff faces that fell away thirty metres on either side. Darren had slowed down, but he was still after them. They slogged on with bursting lungs and aching legs, but they could all clearly see that they were running into a dead end. The path petered out in a rock fall. They could scrabble up it, dangerously; they could turn and face Darren; or they could go over the cliff.

Ben, turning his head to see how far his brother was behind them, caught a glimpse of something that should not be there, a sort of twinkling in the sky. He looked back at it, puzzled, until it dawned on him that it was a star . . . but how could he be seeing stars at midday? It must be an aeroplane gleaming silver in the sun, he thought rapidly, realising in the same moment that the sun was not there any more. Darkness seemed to be falling around him, and when his eyes had adjusted to it, the sky, which a moment ago had been blue and sunny, was black and studded with stars.

He was standing not on the ridge between the two quarries, but on a cliff top that he remembered all too clearly and with dread. He gazed wildly round, catching sight as he did so of strands of silver that ran from star to star. Then he looked back. He could see the scene he had just left as if very far away at the end of a tunnel. He could see the trail bike whizz around the corner, buzzing like a blowfly. It came to a halt, and its tiny rider took off his helmet and looked around in bewilderment.

At the same time he heard Mario give a yell of triumph, and Andrew shouted in his ear, "Jump!"

Ben saw Mario jump. He watched in astonishment as Mario clung to one of the silver strands, pulled himself up on it, and vanished into the sky.

"Jump!" Andrew commanded again, and he and Ben jumped together. Ben felt a moment of terror, as he thought he must plunge downwards. He grabbed in the air.

"Watch out," Andrew hissed in his ear. "It's all right, you're not going to fall. Just hang on and pull yourself up."

Then all three of them were standing together in the first stage of Skymaze.

"Ha!" Mario exulted. "That'll fix Evel Knievel! He can't come after us, can he, Andrew?"

"I don't know," Andrew admitted. "I shouldn't think so. If you haven't played the game you wouldn't know what to look for."

"Sucked in!" Mario crowed. "He'll think we've jumped off the edge. I hope he feels guilty!" Mario dismissed Darren with a last snigger, and then looked intently at Ben. "Heyyyy," he said slowly, as something dawned on him. "Look who we've got with us! The Time Lord himself. Got your watch on you,

Benny boy?"

Ben had been conscious of something cold and heavy on his wrist. He looked down at it and saw the strange face of the unlimited time watch. It had no hands or numbers like a conventional watch. It was more like a screen. A digital 1 appeared on the face of the watch; it dissolved into an infinite number of tiny 1s. Each had a 2 printed on it. One of these swam into close-up and then dissolved into a million tiny 2s. And so on. When it came to 9, the 9s turned into 1s. Ben stared at it. It gave him a sickening feeling of time going on forever.

"Why don't you take it?" he said. "We'll do a swap." But the watch would not come off his wrist, nor could Mario take off the flask of the elixir of healing, which was slung around his neck on a strap.

"Looks like you're stuck with what you chose," Andrew said finally. He did not want to swap anyway, he was more than happy with the flying boots. "So let's go. We should be able to get through the whole thing."

"Do we have to?" Ben said uneasily. Events seemed to have gone beyond his control, and he was starting to wonder how he had got himself into this situation. "It's always the same," he thought in despair. "I never see the moment when I should make a stand, and when I do, it's too late!" Aloud he said, "Can't we go back? Can't we just walk out again?"

"What, and miss the opportunity to solve the maze?" Andrew put on his most persuasive voice and flashed his friendliest smile. "It's fun, honestly. There's nothing dangerous about it. We went all through it before—well, not all the way through, that's what we want to do this time, but through a good part of it. We'll all stay together, okay?"

Mario's methods of persuasion were less subtle. He

took Ben firmly by the arm. "You're coming with us, no argument," he said. "Up you go!"

By now all three boys were familiar enough with the early stages of the game to get through them without anyone losing a life, but as they progressed further it became harder and harder to stay together. The maze became more convoluted and tortuous; several times they had to go back on their tracks because they came to a dead end. Finally, when they had returned for the third time to a particularly nasty cave, Andrew said softly, "I don't like this. I think we're lost!"

"We'll have to go back the way we came," Mario said. "We must have gone wrong earlier on."

"Where are we going *to*?" Ben demanded. "If we don't know where we're going, it doesn't matter if we don't get there."

The others looked at him scornfully. "You've got no sense of adventure, that's your problem," Mario said in disgust.

"Don't you think it's exciting, though?" Andrew enquired. "You're pretty good at it, too," he added.

It was true. With his gymnastics training, Ben was finding, as Elaine had, that he could keep up with and even outstrip the others. He was more agile and had better balance. "Well," he conceded, "I suppose it has its moments—but I'd like it more if I knew the way out! How did you get out before?"

Andrew had hoped Ben wouldn't ask this question. It had been on his mind ever since they had climbed the first ladder. "The game just came to an end. The time elapsed."

"See, we didn't have you with us then," Mario put in, ignoring Andrew's frantic gestures to tell him to shut up.

71

"But the time's not going to elapse, is it?" Ben waved the watch in Mario's face. His voice was rising in alarm. "We've got unlimited time. That means we're stuck in here forever! Didn't you think of that, you pair of maniacs?"

"Calm down! Of course we're not stuck in here forever." Andrew had been going over the rules of the game to reassure himself. "If we lose a life, we find ourselves back on the cliff top where we started off from. Now what's to stop us just walking out?"

"Sounds reasonable to me," Mario said cheerfully. "Let's go on a bit first, though."

"You've never tried it, have you?" Ben went on insistently. "How do you know it works?"

"Just have to hope!" Andrew replied. "I think Mars is right, though. We should explore a bit more first. We might be nearly at the end."

"Or wherever it is we're going," Ben grumbled.

"I think we should go back a bit," Mario said. They carefully negotiated a narrow walkway, ducked under some strange life forms that rose and descended in front of them, and then threw themselves down on the ground as a stream of miniature darts flew rapidly above them.

"This program sure is full of surprises," Mario said in a muffled voice.

"I think it shows a deeply disturbed mind," Andrew muttered.

"Positively warped," Mario agreed.

Ben had been thinking over what Andrew had said earlier. Now he asked them, "What does it feel like when you lose a life?"

"You just sort of black out for a moment. It's nothing bad. Doesn't hurt or anything. When you come to, you're back on the cliff again."

72

"Right," Ben said. He came to a sudden decision. "I'll see you outside," he said. Taking a deep breath, he stood up. For a millisecond he experienced pure panic that the loss of his life would be as devastating as it had been when he had been shot in Space Demons. Then he was afraid no longer. There was a sort of *zapp* as the dart hit him, and everything went black.

When he came to, as Andrew said, he was standing on the cliff top. Above him were the stars and strands of the Skymaze, and behind him was a sort of darkness, at the end of which he could see the minute image of the real world. He walked towards it. As he entered the darkness, he began to feel the lure of the Skymaze. It was as if it did not want him to go. It called on him to stay. He could hear a sort of singing inside him as it begged and pleaded with him. Twice he stopped and looked back, and the starry sky and the web of the maze seemed unutterably beautiful. "I could go back," he thought to himself. "And if I do go back, I'll solve it. I'll get to the end, I know I will." And then he shuddered all over, not entirely with fear.

The real world was growing closer and larger until there was one moment when he was conscious that he was on a threshold. He felt an agonising coldness on his wrist, followed by a sense of lightness as the watch stayed behind in the Skymaze, and he stepped out into the sunshine. The singing in his mind stopped abruptly, leaving him with one piercing flash of regret, and then all he could hear was the birds singing in the valley.

Being on the ridge between the quarries made him reel with vertigo. He wondered how on earth he had run up it so lightly before. He crawled down it on his hands and knees, shaking with exhaustion. Surely the sun was in the wrong place. And why was it so cold? A blackbird whistled sharply as he collapsed under an olive bush. Blackbirds made that sort of noise in the evening, he thought dully to himself. But it had been before lunch when they had gone up to the quarry. He wrapped his arms round his knees and groaned. He couldn't remember when he had felt so terrible. All the agility and lightness he had had in the Skymaze had deserted him. He felt as though he had just run a marathon.

After a few minutes, a scrabbling noise on the gravel made him look back towards the ridge. Andrew and Mario were making their way down it, as slowly and tentatively as he had done. Pale and shaking, they collapsed beside him. They were in no state to look back, but Ben saw the entrance to the Skymaze still there behind them. For one insane moment he wanted to race back into it, but then it faded, and there was nothing there but the evening sky, fast darkening as the sun set, and the sound of magpies and blackbirds.

"Migosh, I think I'm crippled," Andrew moaned.

"You brought it to an end, you jerk!" Mario said to Ben, but he was too exhausted to sound very threatening.

"Just as well," Ben said. "We were in there for hours! We'd better get home. My parents will be wondering what on earth's happened to us."

"At least we know we can always get out," Andrew said, as they struggled to their feet and limped down the hill.

"You're not seriously thinking of going in again!"

"Seems a shame not to!"

"I got out this time," Ben said slowly. "But it didn't want to let me go. It was trying to persuade me to stay."

"Yes, it calls out to you," Andrew said. "It's like it's

74

calling to you all the time. You can't forget about it."

They walked the rest of the way in silence.

When they arrived outside Ben's house, Mario shook himself as though he had just woken from a dream. "Going home," he said briefly. He picked up his bike from the driveway. "You two game to try again?"

"For sure," Andrew said. "I suppose we'll have to play the game again to activate the Skymaze. I'll take the disc home with me now and give you a ring this week. We'll fix a time."

"What about him?" Mario indicated Ben.

"You can ask me directly, you know," Ben said smartly.

"Well?"

"You need me, don't you? I'm better at it than you are, and I've got the unlimited time! You'll never solve it without me." Ben had an unfamiliar sensation of power as he said this. He could tell from the way the others were looking at him that it was true. He had been going to refuse outright to play any more, but that would have meant giving up the sweet feeling of power too soon. He thought he would keep them in suspense for a while.

"I'll think about it," he said casually. "I probably won't . . . but, you never know, I might!"

CHAPTER SIX

"What I want to know," Darren said suspiciously to Ben the following morning as they were leaving for school, "is where the hell you all disappeared to."

Darren had kept a very low profile the night before while Ben and Andrew received a stern lecture from both sets of parents on sensible and responsible behaviour. Keith and Marjorie Freeman had been waiting at Ben's house for a couple of hours to take Andrew home, and though nobody liked to admit it, they were all starting to get worried. When the boys did finally turn up, so spaced out they could hardly walk, everyone jumped to the worst of conclusions. Ben and Andrew could do little to clear up the confusion.

"We were just up at the quarry," Ben said lightly to Darren. He was still feeling exhausted from the adventure in the Skymaze, but he also felt surprisingly pleased with himself, as though he had proved to himself something basic that from now on would change the way he looked at the world.

"You freaking well weren't! I searched the whole place. You'd all disappeared completely." Darren turned and grabbed Ben by the shirt collar. "Something's going on, isn't it? What are you and those other creeps up to?"

"You'll never find out!" Ben replied. "Now let go of me, or I'll dob you in about the bike. You shouldn't have been up there in the first place."

Rather to his surprise, Darren did let go. As Ben walked quickly away, Darren stood for a moment staring after him.

"We must have rattled him all right," Ben thought with satisfaction. Knowing about the Skymaze, having been in it and explored it, gave him a strong feeling of being one up on Darren. He felt at least five centimetres taller as he strolled into the school yard.

At recess he told Elaine about what had happened. As he described the Skymaze, his eyes were sparkling, and he kept laughing with excitement.

She looked at him suspiciously. "You really liked it, didn't you?"

"Well, in a way. It was pretty exciting. Didn't you think so?"

"Uuunnh!" she responded, with a curious noise that started out as "No way" and ended up as "You bet!" They looked at each other and laughed maniacally.

"We must be crazy," Elaine said weakly. She had been trying not to think about the Skymaze. She had the feeling she might have dreamed about it, and it was lurking somewhere in her unconscious mind, trying in some way to entice her back. One moment she was determined to resist it; the next she couldn't wait to have another shot at it. She got to her feet, put the empty Fruit Box she had been drinking on the ground, and jumped on it. It exploded with a satisfying bang.

"Throw it in the bin, you litter bug," Ben told her. He got up too as Mario came quickly up to them. "Where've you been, Mars? Recess is nearly over."

"Playing poker in the classroom. Then I got waylaid by Ms Riley. I hadn't done the homework for English. I was so wiped out when I got home last night I just collapsed in bed."

"Did you get into trouble?"

"Course not! My parents don't care what time I get in. They never bother about anything I do any more." There was a touch of bravado about the way he said this that made both Elaine and Ben suspect he was not being quite honest about it, but Mario simply continued, "Cool fun, though, wasn't it?"

"I suppose, if you like that sort of thing!" Ben said with feigned casualness. "Personally I can take it or leave it."

"What about you, Mad Mouse?" Mario looked teasingly at Elaine. "You missed out on a great day yesterday. It was unreal!"

"I had better things to do," Elaine replied promptly. "Actually, I had a very important telephone call from Shaz Christie—of course, you wouldn't know who that is, not being interested in anything but your dumb games."

"I've heard of her," Ben said, impressed. "We went to see one of her shows at Come Out this year. It was pretty radical."

"Well, make sure you see her show at the Festival next year," Elaine replied rather smugly. "Because I'm going to be in it!"

"No kidding!" Ben was thrilled. "That's fantastic!"

"You want to come along with me to the rehearsal on Friday? She needs a couple more boys, she said so. You could be in it too!"

"Get away, I'm not good enough."

"You don't know what she's looking for. You can do a bit of gym, you're not bad." Then, because she was very conscious of Mario standing next to them, silent and scowling, Elaine said to him, "Why don't you come along too?"

Mario said something rather rude about the suggestion, and the siren sounded for the end of recess.

"I've got to run," Ben said. "I've got a maths class in the senior school, and I'm always late. See you at lunch!"

"Why don't you come with us?" Elaine repeated challengingly as Mario walked along with her to her next class.

"I thought you might like to come to the movies with me on Friday," he replied, giving her an unreadable look from under his dark lashes.

Elaine was astonished. "You mean you're asking me out?"

"Why not? I like you!"

"You've got a funny way of showing it." She was still resentful over his behaviour in the Skymaze on Saturday night.

"Awww!" he exclaimed. "That was a game! You've got to play to win, haven't you? That doesn't mean I don't like you."

"Well, if you like me so much, come with me to the rehearsal."

"You must be joking! You wouldn't catch me prancing around looking like a poofter!"

"You're so stupid," Elaine replied, enraged. "You'd never really do anything for me, would you? You just want to say you've got a girlfriend and look all macho! Well, forget it. I'm not interested in being anyone's girlfriend."

"I thought you liked me," he said indignantly.

"I'm not saying I don't like you. I like a lot of

79

people—they're my friends. But that doesn't mean I want to go out with them, or be their girlfriend. Just because you like me doesn't give you any rights over me! Anyway, I've got to go, I'm late for tech. studies already. See you later."

Mario, always late for classes, did not hurry, but Elaine ran as fast as she could, not so much because she was late, but rather as if she could run away from Mario altogether. She didn't like the way he had made her feel: that she was in some way obliged to respond because he fancied her. She was quite happy just to be friends with him, and boy, did he need friends, even though he pretended to be so tough! But she was definitely not going to get involved with him. "Auntie Jan was right," she thought, as she slipped into the tech. studies room and made a rapid apology to Mr Cartwright. "He's nothing but trouble." Then she put him firmly out of her mind and thought about Shaz Christie instead. She felt like leaping round the room and turning somersaults on the benches. She was going to be in a show, she was being paid for it, she was being paid to dance!

"This is the start!" she said to herself as she worked on the polisher with John Ferrone. "This is the start of my career. I am definitely going to be famous!"

The week went slowly by. Paul Freeman had a virus which kept him in bed for a couple of days, and off Andrew's back. Andrew and Mario, on opposite sides of the city, spent the days longing impatiently for the weekend when they could get together and play Skymaze, and the nights dreaming about it. Ben got into more trouble that week than he had in his entire life, and couldn't understand why everyone kept picking on him. Elaine had a phone call from her father in Darwin.

It was Thursday night and she was already in bed when the phone rang. Mrs Fields called to her from the living-room.

"Elly, you aren't asleep, are you? Your dad's on the phone."

Elaine leaped out of bed. Her father occasionally sent her postcards and letters, and he phoned every couple of weeks, but she hadn't heard from him for a while. She realised that she was longing to hear his voice, and longing to tell him about Shaz.

"Dad?" she cried down the phone. "Listen, I've got some great news."

His voice came crackling down the line. "You tell me yours first, honey, then I'll tell you mine."

When she had breathlessly poured out all the details, he was silent for a couple of nerve-racking moments.

"Well, aren't you pleased?" she demanded. "I fixed it all up by myself. It's what I've always wanted to do, and I made it happen!"

"Yeah, of course I'm pleased. I'm thrilled for you. But it kind of knocks my news on the head. I've been offered a job in Papua New Guinea, and I thought you'd like to come with me. It'd be such a great experience to travel a bit, see another way of life . . ." His voice seemed to disappear somewhere in the vast distance between the Fields' house and Darwin.

Elaine could feel her heart growing tight and small in her chest. "When are you going?" she asked.

"Early next month. I figured you could fly up here and meet me. It doesn't matter if you miss the rest of this term, does it? . . . But of course, if you really want to do this dance thing, you'll want to stay put."

"What about Christmas? Would you come back

for that?"

"I dunno. Might be able to swing it."

Elaine was so caught up in the idea of working with Shaz that she didn't even stop to think about it. "I've got to stay here," she said firmly. "Sorry and all that, but I've just got to. You do understand, don't you?"

"Sure," he said, but his voice sounded more and more distant, and as soon as Elaine had put the phone down, she was tormented by doubt.

She slept badly and dreamed exhausting dreams of pursuing something or somebody through an endless, tortuous maze, wanting desperately to catch up with it, but never able to. In the morning she snapped at Mrs Fields for telling her to take a coat with her, and then she had an argument with Linda on the way to school. It was over something quite trivial, but Linda was still annoyed with Elaine for disappearing with Mario at the Show, and she stalked off to the Lutheran college she attended without saying goodbye. By the time Elaine got on the bus with Ben after school that afternoon to go into the city, she was tense and on edge, worried too about the coming rehearsal, and afraid that Shaz would not want her after all.

"I nearly didn't make it," Ben gasped as they collapsed panting on the back seat of the bus, having had to run a hundred metres to beat it to the stop. "Right up to the last moment Mum was saying, 'I don't know that this is a good idea.' Apparently Shaz Christie has got a bit of a weird reputation, and one of the teachers at Mum's school said she wouldn't let her children associate with her. But Dad pointed out how it was so good for me to have outside interests, et cetera, et cetera, and they'd always encouraged us to be independent, and since you were going too, it would probably be all right as long as we stayed together.

They would have driven us, but they're going to the theatre tonight and they didn't have time. But Darren's going to pick us up afterwards and bring us home"—here he put on his mother's voice—"'so we're not hanging around the city late at night and getting into trouble'. We've got to meet him at the central car park just next to the studios. He's gone to the five o'clock session at the movies."

"You'd think they'd all be overjoyed that we were doing something constructive and earning some money," Elaine replied. "Auntie Jan was a bit dubious about it too. I think she was about to change her mind, only I said you were coming with me, and then she thought that made it all right."

"She hasn't heard about my growing reputation, luckily," Ben said with a laugh. "Good thing she didn't check with my mum. I've had a really weird week. I seem to have been in strife with everyone. Ever since Sunday I've been feeling like taking everyone on. I've had dozens of fights with Darren. We nearly came to blows last night. Do you know," he turned round in the seat and looked seriously at Elaine, "I think everyone has been taking advantage of me all my life. My family just thinks I'll agree to anything. Everyone pushes me around all the time. I suddenly noticed it. And when I don't let them boss me, they accuse me of being difficult!"

"It's true," Elaine said. "You've always been too nice to everyone. You always do what they ask you to. You should stand up for yourself a bit more." She sighed. "If only it wasn't so hard. No one likes you if you stand up for yourself. I've had a rotten week too." She gazed out of the bus window for a few moments, and he thought she was not going to say any more, but then she turned back to him and said, all in a rush, "Do you think they really like me or are they just doing the right thing and being kind to me?"

"The Fields?"

"Mmm." She made a self-deprecating face and went on, "I wouldn't blame them if they didn't like me. I don't think I've been very easy to get on with this week. I feel awful about it, really. They try to be kind, and I'm always thinking, 'Oh, you're just doing that to be kind; you don't really mean it . . . .'." She looked straight ahead, out of the front window of the bus. "I miss my dad," she said abruptly. "I wish I was still living with him."

"Perhaps he'll come back and settle down here."

"That's what I've been hoping, but now it looks as though there's no chance of that." Earlier she had decided she didn't want to talk about it to anyone, but now she had started she found she couldn't stop. "He phoned up last night. He's been offered a job in Papua New Guinea, starting next month. He wanted me to go with him; he'll be away for six months, and it's too far to keep coming over to visit. But I told him about being in the show, and I said I'd rather stay here till it was over. Now I don't know if I did the right thing. I wish I could see him and talk to him about it." She was starting to feel terrible about it. She had a sudden gut longing for his physical presence, so strong it almost brought tears to her eyes.

Ben looked at her sympathetically. It occurred to him that he liked her more than anyone he knew. The realisation was fascinating; it made him feel extremely happy in a way he had never felt before. Without thinking about what he was doing, he put his arm round her and gave her a spontaneous and friendly hug. "Don't go away," he said. "Stay here. We'll do the show together, if I get in. We can do lots of things together. It's going to be great."

"That is just crappy!" Shaz Christie swore at the group of children gathered in the studio. They had been working for an hour, doing warm-ups and some basic tumbling, and now she was trying to get them to do improvisations. Because they didn't know each other and were new to the whole situation, they were all self-conscious and giggly, and one or two of them were being downright silly.

Shaz ran her hand through her black-and-silver hair in frustration. The stud in her nose was now a black pearl, and she was dressed entirely in black. She glared at them as if she could transfer energy to them. "Don't waste my time by giving me garbage. And don't waste your own time by not being honest. I want to get at what's real inside you, not the phoney rubbish you think you're meant to be producing. Get into your pairs and let's try it again."

After a few moments she groaned again. "Don't be too literal," she yelled at them. "I don't want stories. I want feelings."

"What's she getting at?" Ben muttered to Elaine. "I don't know if I want to do this after all!"

"I think I know what she's getting at, it's just that I find it so hard to do," Elaine said. It needed music, she was thinking, and lighting, and special costumes. She could see it in her head, as a finished production, but now they were only working with the bare bones, their own bodies, and that was the hardest part.

Images formed slowly in her head, images of fears that usually lay deeply buried, nightmares she had had, movies and TV programs that had terrified her. To reproduce them in movement, she had to allow them to take her over. She made a few tentative shapes and

85

positions, then she tried them out again.

"What are you doing?" Ben asked.

"Think of the images," she replied. "Think of the pictures the fears make in your head, and then let them move you."

Ben was silent for a few moments, and then he exclaimed, "Oh, I think I get it!" He had one particular nightmare in which someone you think can be trusted turns out to be a fiend, and he had seen it again recently in a horror movie. He put his brother's face on this image and let the feeling move him.

"That's getting more like it," Shaz said, sounding faintly surprised. She had come over to the corner where Elaine and Ben were working, and was watching them. "Show the others," she commanded. "Don't talk about it, just do it. Let it flow. It'll happen, it's happening already."

Shaz was pretty alarming, Ben thought afterwards. The way she challenged them to be real and up-front all the time scared him silly. But she gave them lots of energy too. She was so unusual and unpredictable.

"What did you think of it?" Elaine asked as they stood at the kerb among a crowd of late-night shoppers, waiting to cross the road.

"It was okay," Ben replied. Looking back, he realised he had enjoyed it. Even though parts of it had been painfully difficult, it had been exciting too, and challenging. And the discovery that he was good at it had been fantastic. He had never particularly considered dancing as a thing to do, but now that Elaine had dragged him into it he could see that it had definite possibilities. "Darren'll laugh himself sick," a small voice suggested in his head. "Stuff Darren," he replied to himself.

"So you reckon you'll be in it?"

"Wouldn't miss it for anything!"

"Great!" Elaine said, delighted.

"Come on, we'd better hurry." Ben took advantage of the fact that they were crossing the road to put his arm across her shoulder. "It's after eight and Darren will have been waiting for ages."

Once across the road, he scanned the crowd anxiously. "He said he'd meet us down here. I can't see him anywhere. The movie must be over. Let's go up into the car park and see if we can find the car."

They took the lift to the top floor and began to work their way downwards. The car park was fairly full, but there weren't many people around; it was too early for the late-night shoppers to be going home, and in between sessions for the cinemas. The elation Ben and Elaine had felt at the end of the rehearsal began to seep out of them.

Elaine shivered. "Creepy place, isn't it?"

Acting out their fears earlier had brought unspoken things to the surface of their minds. The place looked as though it might be full of ghosts or sex maniacs or both. Ben jumped as a car swept past them. "Perhaps we'd better go back down," he suggested, trying to make it sound like a sensible thing to do and not as if he was scared.

"Okay," Elaine agreed, rather thankfully.

They were crossing the car lane to get to the lift when an engine revved up in the dark behind them. It sounded familiar to Ben, and he turned to look. "There's the car!" he said with relief, and he started waving and jumping up and down to attract Darren's attention.

The car came towards them, but it came at speed, its headlights full on and blinding.

"Slow down, maniac," Elaine muttered, as it

screeched to a halt beside them. Ben tried to open the door, but it was locked.

"Open the door, Darren!" he yelled.

Darren wound the window down a fraction and put his lips close to the gap.

"Hunter!" he whispered, softly but menacingly. His eyes were sparkling as though it was a huge joke.

"Don't be stupid! You're supposed to be taking us home. Now let us in. I'll tell Dad!"

Elaine tried the back door, but that was locked too.

Darren wound up the window again, and put his foot on the accelerator. Ben leaped back as the car jolted forward. "Idiot!" he yelled.

"What's he doing?" Elaine demanded incredulously.

"It's a stupid game he makes me play. We've played it ever since I was little. It's called Hunter, and I have to run away and he has to get me. Sometimes it goes on for days, and I never know when he's going to pounce. That's why I try and stay clear of him. He's quite mad!"

"You're the one who's mad to let him push you around all the time," Elaine said disgustedly. "Why d'you let him?"

Ben did not have time to answer. His mother's Laser, with Darren at the wheel, had completed a circuit of the level and was returning at top speed.

"He's not going to run us over," Elaine said. "Just stand still." But as the car showed no sign of stopping, they both lost their nerve and turned and ran up the laneway, towards the roof level.

"Pretend we're running away," Elaine gasped. "Then we'll get the lift down and get the bus home. That'll teach him!"

But even though they were pretending they were running away, it was still terrifying. "It's just like what I was acting before," Ben thought. "When someone you know suddenly turns nasty, it is so scary. Especially when you're not sure if it's just a game or not." Darren was mad at him for all the things that had happened between them that week; he suspected Ben was up to something mysterious; and he was now taking advantage of the old game to find out more and get even with him.

The Laser was at their heels, but it had to slow down to negotiate the ninety-degree bend as they reached the top level. Ben and Elaine ducked behind the parked cars and looked wildly around.

"Where to now?" Ben gasped.

"Over to the lift," Elaine panted back, and then she said, with a note of panic in her voice, "It's awfully dark up here! I can't see a thing!"

Ben made a grab for where her hand should have been, and found it. "Don't let go," he said. "We must stay together!" The darkness was falling all around them, but over their heads he could catch a glimpse of a familiar shimmering. One by one the stars appeared, huge and almost within reach in the dark velvety sky.

He had not thought consciously about the Skymaze all day, but now it had appeared in front of them like a giant web, it seemed inevitable that it should be there. It was as though he was on the rebound again and was ricocheting into it—almost, he thought, with another twinge of fear, as though it had been waiting for them.

"Andrew and Mars must have played it again," he said wonderingly to Elaine as they walked slowly forwards. "They must have activated it. But why didn't they warn us? They'll be furious if we get in it and they don't."

"Serves them right!" Elaine retorted. "Anyone would think the whole thing belonged to them!"

"But it doesn't," she thought. "It belongs to us all."

She also had a feeling of inevitability about the Sky-maze being there, as though she had dreamed about it once too often, and now her dream had come true. She realised she was glad to see it again. It seemed like a haven. "Let's hide in here! Darren can't follow us. We'll get out later when he's given up and gone home."

Ben looked back. He saw the headlights of the Laser shining in the distance as if at the end of a long, dark tunnel. Faced with the alternative of confronting Darren and continuing with the crazy game of Hunter, he decided that the Skymaze looked almost attractive. "It'll serve him right!" he agreed. "He'll have to go home and tell Mum and Dad he lost us!"

He swung himself up on a strand of the Skymaze, and Elaine followed.

They had meant to stay on the first level and wait until it seemed safe to leave. They had not meant to go on up into the Skymaze. But as they stood at the foot of the silver ladder and looked around, marvelling at the luminous complexity of all the facets of the maze spiralling away into the distance, Ben said suddenly, "I'd love to get to the centre of it, wouldn't you?"

"What do you think it is?" Elaine replied dreamily. She sounded so unlike her normal jumpy self that Ben turned to look at her. Her eyes shone with the silver light of the maze, and her hair glowed with an unearthly burnished colour. Her face, which was usually sharp and wary, had softened so that she looked almost beautiful. It alarmed Ben enormously.

"What's the matter?" he hissed.

"Nothing's the matter," she replied, turning her silver eyes very slowly towards him. "I feel very good all of a sudden. I feel as if I can do anything I want." She gestured towards the intricate spirals. "I feel as if any of that is possible. I can do any of it, go anywhere."

She fell silent. The prospect seemed too splendid to put into words. Ben felt a tremor of excitement begin in his stomach and ripple through him all the way to his toes.

"I bet we could do it," he exclaimed. "I bet we could get through it. We're much better at it than the others! And I've got unlimited time!"

"That would show them all," he exulted inwardly. It seemed to be the culmination of all his attempts to stand up for himself. It would prove once and for all that he could do things on his own. It would be one in the eye for Andrew, all right, and the others who were always bossing him around—Mario, Darren, the lot of them!

Elaine gave him a long, searching look. She was not smiling but her eyes were alight with excitement too. Without speaking, she took hold of the first rung of the ladder and began to climb.

For both of them this was only their second time in the Skymaze, and yet they were both aware of finding it altered. As they progressed slowly, their excitement began to wane.

"Was it as hard as this when you were in with the others?" Ben asked, as they narrowly escaped falling from a treacherous bridge.

"I can't really remember," Elaine said. She looked out over the edge and saw the distant arms of the maze. "We're never going to get out there," she exclaimed, discouraged by the distance, and by something else she could not quite name. "It feels a lot more creepy, that's for sure!" She glanced anxiously behind her. "You know that stuff we did with Shaz? All that inner fear

91

stuff? I keep kind of seeing things like that."

Then she shrieked as something rose beside them and hovered over them. They both shrank back against the wall, paralysed with fear, though neither of them could describe exactly what it was they were afraid of. It was as though, having lured them in, the Skymaze was now using their own secret terrors against them.

Ben grabbed Elaine by the arm. "This is horrible," he whispered. "Let's go back!"

The creature sank away again, with a faint, gibbering moan.

Elaine gave a gasp of relief. "What a revolting thing! What on earth was it?"

"I don't really know," Ben replied in a shaky voice. "At least, I think I've seen it before somewhere, but I'd rather not think about it! What'll we do? Shall we just go back? I don't want to be killed by one of those things. I don't like the look of them at all!"

"Me neither!" Elaine agreed. She looked again in frustration at the more distant spirals of the maze. They seemed to be calling to her, tempting her. "You know," she said, "I can feel the way inside me, but I can't seem to find the right path. I know we can do it if only . . . if only . . ." She fell silent, shaking her head as if to clear it.

"If only what?" Ben prompted her after a moment.

"It's not only that it's got harder to go forward because of those terrifying things. I feel as if there's something missing, something I need. Like you've got the watch. I need something like that."

"You never got to choose anything, did you?" Ben exclaimed. "It would be something that you need to choose in the grotto—some other object that's going to help us get through the maze. We probably can't solve it without that. We'd better get back."

"Then," he was thinking, "we will play the game again. Elaine can choose something—whatever it is—and we'll come back together!"

The idea filled them with excitement and hope. For the Skymaze had taken hold of them, and they would have no peace until they had solved it.

CHAPTER SEVEN

Mario took the bus over to Andrew's house the following morning. His eyes nearly fell out of his head when he came to the gate of the North Adelaide mansion, and he had to light a cigarette to calm his nerves.

"Hey, put that out," Andrew said hastily when he opened the door. "Mum'll have a fit if she sees you smoking. She's given it up, and no one's allowed to smoke in the house!"

"You've come up in the world," Mario observed sarcastically, throwing his cigarette into the camellias and stepping into the panelled entrance hall.

Andrew was not in the mood for social chit-chat. "Come on," he said, hustling Mario down the corridor towards the back of the house and the computer room. "We won't have very long. My stepfather's taken Paul to his archery lesson. They'll be back before twelve. Let's get on with the game."

"You've really got it made, haven't you?" Mario said bitterly, looking round. "What did you do to deserve it? Everything's always going to work out all right for you. You've just got to hang in there long enough and you'll float effortlessly to the top."

"Don't make me feel guilty," Andrew replied. "It's not my fault!"

"It's not my fault either," Mario retorted. "It's not my fault that I'm never going to get anywhere unless I look out for myself."

"You can always take up a life of crime," Andrew said lightly.

"Get stuffed!"

"You're in a nice mood!"

"I've had a crummy week. All my weeks are crummy. My whole life is crummy. I'm sick of it all."

Andrew was silent. He felt they were getting on to very dangerous ground. "Come on," he said awkwardly. "Let's play the game."

A brief smile lit up Mario's normally unsmiling face. "Yeah! The answer to all life's problems."

Andrew switched the computer on and put the disc in. Then he plugged in both joysticks while he waited for the program to load. The cliff top came up on the screen, but the game did not respond any further to the controls.

"What's happened to it?" Andrew muttered, moving the joystick backwards, forwards and side-ways. "Something's gone wrong."

There was a flicker on the screen, and a message printed out along the bottom.

STATE OF PLAY: LEVEL 3: SKYMAZE ACTIVATED. PALE GUARDIANS ACTIVATED. CONTROL PLAY IMPOSSIBLE.

"What's that mean?" Mario said, staring at it intently.

"Someone else must have played it," Andrew said incredulously. He couldn't believe it. Someone had already done what he had been anxiously waiting all week to do. He swore furiously. "Someone's played it,

95

and taken one of the objects." Then he pushed back his chair so violently that it fell over with a crash. "Paul! It must be Paul! He was home from school this week. He said he was ill. I knew he was faking it, I told Mum and Keith he was, but they wouldn't believe it. He faked it, and when I was at school he went into my room and found the game!"

He was staring at Mario as all the implications hit him. Paul had never played Space Demons; he shouldn't have played Skymaze. He didn't know not to touch the gun. Now he had activated not only the Skymaze, but also the Pale Guardians. Andrew didn't know what they were, but he very definitely didn't like the sound of them.

"Sheesh!" he swore again. He was vaguely aware that the phone was ringing, but he was still staring open-mouthed and horrified at Mario when his mother came down the corridor calling urgently, "Andrew! Andrew!"

The door flew open as Marjorie came in with a rush. She stopped suddenly when she saw Mario.

"Oh, I didn't know you were here!" She did not look very pleased about it, but she did not say anything else to him. Instead she spoke rapidly to Andrew. "It's Mrs Challis on the phone. Have you any idea where Ben is today?"

Andrew shook his head. "I haven't even spoken to him since last Sunday. Why?"

"Oh, Andrew!" Marjorie picked up the chair from the floor and sank down on it. "They're so worried. Ben didn't come home last night. He went to a rehearsal in the city with some girl he knows, and neither of them came back!"

"Oh no!" Andrew said. Things began to piece themselves together in his mind. He looked at Mario.

Mario looked back and nodded slightly. He knew just what Andrew was thinking, because he was thinking the same thing.

"Apparently the girl was really upset—her father is going to Papua New Guinea. She lives with the Fields. You know, Mrs Fields is the school secretary . . ."

"Yes, I know," Andrew said impatiently. "It's Elaine Taylor, I know her."

"Well, Mrs Fields thinks there's a chance Elaine is trying to get to her father. He's up north somewhere at the moment. She was quite distressed yesterday, apparently, and then Helen Challis said Ben hasn't been himself all week. And after Sunday," she paused and looked accusingly at Andrew, "they don't know what's going on."

"No, they don't," Andrew thought. "But I do. At least, I can make a darned good guess."

His mother said anxiously, "I must get back to Helen. So you don't know anything? Ben didn't say anything to you?"

"No," Andrew replied. "I don't think she should worry though. I'm sure they're not far away, and they'll be back soon." He gave her what he hoped was an encouraging grin, but she took it the wrong way.

"Oh, Andrew," she said crossly. "Can't you take anything seriously?" She gave him an exasperated look and left the room.

"You're thinking what I'm thinking, aren't you?" Mario demanded immediately.

"Yeah. Don't ask me how or why, but my guess is they're trapped in the Skymaze. That idiot Paul!"

"But why did they go in?" Mario said as if to himself. "I didn't think they were that keen to try it again."

"Perhaps they couldn't help it," Andrew said. "You know how it grows on you. I've been thinking about it

97

all week. It's like it's trying to suck you back in."

Mario nodded. He knew the feeling all too well. "What do we do now, then?"

"We'll have to go and look for them," Andrew replied, making it sound like the easiest thing in the world.

"Well, sure, but where the heck do we start?"

"We'll have to think it out logically," Andrew said, trying to do just that. "Let's go and find out some more from Mum."

Marjorie's movements were tense and anxious as she made herself a cup of coffee in the kitchen, and her state of mind was not improved by Mario, who managed to slouch by the door both silently and aggressively while Andrew questioned her. She made Mario tense too, and an awkward silence had fallen when they heard the Lancia pull into the garage. A few moments later Keith and Paul came into the house. They clattered into the kitchen, talking and laughing excitedly.

"This boy!" Keith exclaimed, his arm draped affectionately over Paul's shoulders. "What a champion! William Tell lives again!" Then he registered the unusual level of anxiety in the kitchen, and said quickly to Marjorie, "What's wrong?"

"One of Andrew's friends, Ben Challis, didn't come home last night. His parents are desperate. I was just talking to Helen on the phone."

"Is there anything we can do to help them?" Keith switched effortlessly into his professional role. "Have they told the police?"

Marjorie told him as much as she knew, while Andrew, Mario and Paul eyed each other off suspiciously.

Mario and Paul disliked each other on sight. Andrew had every reason to be furious with his stepbrother just then, but he was struggling to control his anger. He would deal with Paul properly later. Right now he had to think out a plan of action, and he had to do it quickly. While the excitement in the kitchen was buzzing around him, his brain was seething with ideas.

Marjorie finished her story, and said to her husband, "This is Andrew's friend, Mario. I don't think you've met him before." She couldn't help making it sound as if she hoped he never would again, either. However, Keith was prepared to take a friendly interest in Mario.

"Ah, the great games player," he remarked cheerfully, as he held out his hand. "Good to meet you at last."

Mario regarded the hand with deep suspicion, and gave Keith a swift up-and-down glance. He stuck his own hands firmly in his pockets and muttered, "Howdy!" Then he looked intently at the floor.

"Paul just came first in his archery trials," Keith explained. "He has a good chance of being selected for the State team."

Mario gave a non-committal grunt and looked unimpressed.

"Have you ever done any archery?" Keith enquired.

"Bows and arrows?" Mario replied scornfully. "It always looks kind of dumb to me."

Keith laughed. "Robin Hood and all that? I know what you mean. But it's good fun, and excellent training for co-ordination. You should try it some time. You look as if you'd have a good eye."

"I'm a good shot," Mario told him, looking up for the first time. "I always win things at the Show."

Andrew, who was listening to the conversation with

99

half an ear, suddenly registered that Keith and Mario were actually talking to each other. "He sounds as though he's really interested in Mars," he admitted to himself. "I wonder if he's just putting it on. If he is, he's pretty good at it. He's actually got Mars to tell him something about himself." Then he dismissed the thought and began to put his plans into action.

"Congratulations!" he said smoothly to Paul, giving him a brilliant smile and punching him on the shoulder in an entirely friendly fashion. "Let's all go out to lunch and celebrate! Can we, Keith?"

"Great idea, Andy! I'll have to duck out, though, this time. I'm supposed to be at a seminar this afternoon. I've just got time for a sandwich before I go."

"That's all right," Andrew said, thinking that in fact it was even better. "Mars and I'll take Paul to the Hamburger House." He winked sideways at Mario, who gave him a flicker of a wink back. Andrew felt a curious feeling, almost of gratitude. "That's the great thing about Mars," he thought. "You don't have to explain things to him. He always knows what's going on." The Hamburger House was right next to the multi-storey car park where Ben and Elaine had been meant to meet Darren the night before. It seemed as good a place as any to start looking.

"Actually . . ." Paul started to say, but Andrew did not let him continue.

"You're not going to veto, are you?" he said. It sounded pleading to the adults' ears, but Paul caught the warning beneath the words. He said something rude about Andrew under his breath, his face turned away so his father would not hear.

"Of course he's not going to veto," Keith said encouragingly. "It's a terrific idea. I wish I could come too, but I'll shout you instead. What about you, darling?" he said to Marjorie.

She shook her head. "I think they'll have more fun without me," she said with a laugh.

"Don't try and fool us. The Hamburger House isn't your idea of a celebration," Paul told her, rather sourly.

"Just give me five minutes and I'll drop you off on my way." Keith pulled open the fridge door and started making himself a sandwich.

Andrew gave his mother a hug, partly to remind Keith and Paul that she was his mother, something he thought they tended to forget, and partly because he could see that she was really upset about Ben and Elaine. "We'll have a scout round for Ben afterwards," he said. "Don't worry, they'll be back tonight, I'm sure."

"Andrew, if you know anything, you must tell us," she said urgently.

He did not reply, not sure what to say without either giving away the secret of Skymaze, or lying. He glanced quickly at his stepfather, who was munching through his sandwich of roast beef and pickles, apparently not taking any notice. He couldn't help wondering if Keith suspected anything. It seemed so obvious to Andrew that all three boys were trying to hide some very peculiar feelings. Keith gave him a look of bland innocence in return.

If Keith did have any suspicions, he did not mention them on the drive to the city. Instead, he talked to Mario about Italian cars and made jokes with Paul. Strangely enough, Paul did not find them very funny.

"Are we really going in here?" Mario said in surprise, as Andrew headed towards the entrance of the hamburger restaurant. "I thought we'd go straight up to the car park."

"We may as well have something to eat," Andrew replied. "I'm starving. And anyway, we've got some things to discuss, haven't we, Paul?" He gave his step-brother a meaningful glare and a dig in the ribs.

"That's news to me," Paul replied. "I'd like it to go on the record that I'm here unwillingly and under protest. I'm going to eat my hamburger as fast as possible and depart."

Mario regarded him with interest, as if he was some kind of unusual specimen. "Do you always talk like that?"

"Oh, I can talk your language too," Paul said scornfully, and proceeded to demonstrate under his breath.

"Lay off," Andrew said uneasily. "They'll chuck us out." Paul snorted even more scornfully, but went towards the counter and ordered hamburgers, chips and drinks. When they were all sitting at a window table, Andrew broke the hostile silence by saying, "You'd better tell us what you did."

Paul put down his half-eaten hamburger and took a swig of Coke. He looked coolly back at Andrew over the edge of the paper cup. "I haven't the faintest idea what you're referring to."

"I'm referring to a particular computer game called Skymaze, which belongs to me, and which I told you not to play and which you took and played."

"You can't prove that," Paul began, quite unmoved by the anger in Andrew's voice.

"That's where you're wrong. We can prove it. You know how? Because you didn't know how to play and you did the wrong thing."

"Can't you read?" Mario put in with a sneer. "Didn't you see the game said you can only play it if you've played Space Demons?"

Paul did not say anything. He took up his hamburger, looked at it, and put it down again without touching it.

"You took the gun, didn't you?" Andrew went on insistently. "You shouldn't have done that."

"You should have let me play it," Paul replied sullenly. "You should have told me about it instead of being so selfish and secretive. I only wanted to see what it was like."

"You've really made a mess of things," Andrew said in disgust. "Why do you poke your big nose into everything all the time?"

Paul was recovering some of his aplomb. "You're being very mysterious about it. What am I supposed to have done anyway? Spoilt your game? You've got heaps of others. Or you can ask Marjorie to get you another one. She gives you everything you want."

"You don't understand, do you?" Andrew leaned over the table to emphasise the point. "It's not just an ordinary game. What you do when you play it counts. And then it comes alive. It's not just a game. It's real."

"Aren't you getting a bit old for fantasies?" Paul said with contempt.

"It is not fantasy," Mario told him impatiently. For a moment all three boys were silent while the hubbub of the restaurant rose and fell around them. Then Mario continued, "You'd better tell us exactly what you did."

Paul took a bite of his hamburger and chewed for a few seconds before answering. "This doesn't taste very nice," he complained.

"It'll taste even worse in a minute," Mario said, "because I'm going to put it on the floor and stamp on it if you don't talk."

"Oh! Oh!" Paul exclaimed, pretending to be terrified. "All right, I'll talk, I'll talk! Please don't hit me!" He cowered down and tried to hide under the table.

Andrew gave him a light kick on the shin. "Stop mucking around!"

Paul took another bite of the hamburger. He didn't want to say any more to the others, but at the same time he was fascinated by the game. Since he had played it, he had dreamed about it in strange ways. It felt almost as if it was talking to him in his sleep. Despite his apparent contempt for Andrew and Mario, he was secretly intrigued by what they had told him. The thought of the game coming alive sent a tingle of excitement down his spine. And the excitement hooked on to something less innocent inside him, a feeling that he could somehow teach Andrew a lesson and get even with him once and for all.

"Okay," he said slowly, watching their faces carefully, "I'll tell you what happened. I played the game. I didn't take any notice of the warning, because I couldn't see how the game would know one way or the other—"

"Did the character on the screen look like you?" Andrew interrupted.

Paul shook his head. "Not that I noticed. It was a storm-trooper type of figure, with a very pale face and hands."

"A Pale Guardian?" Mario wondered. "The game *did* know. It can recognise you in some way. If you've been through Space Demons it knows you. It didn't know you, and so you activated another stage."

"Then what happened?" Andrew said, fighting down the desire to call Paul all the worst names he could think of.

"I got all the way up to the magic grotto, and the computer said I could choose something to help me through the Skymaze. There were two things, one was a sort of compass, I think it called it a true sense of direction, and the other was a gun—the power to defend yourself by force. I remember that because . . ." He broke off, not sure how much he was giving away.

"Because what?" Andrew questioned impatiently.

"Because I keep hearing that in my head. All mixed up with being a Pale Guardian, and having to defend myself." He shook his head abruptly, not wanting to go on and tell them that he now also felt compelled to defend something else; he was still not sure what it was, but the compulsion was making him more and more hostile. "Happy now?" he sneered at them. He wanted to get away from them, but at the same time he had to know what the game was all about.

"That's just what we figured," Andrew said. "Is that all? The computer didn't say anything else? Nothing else happened?"

"Oh, I forgot." Paul gathered up the remnants of his meal in a single swoop and stood up. "It did say something else."

"What?" both the other boys exclaimed at once.

"It said, 'Andrew Hayford is a moron!'." Paul slung the rubbish into the disposal chute, and gave them a derisive wave. "Thanks for the celebration lunch, I don't think! I'll leave you two to your childish pursuits. Hope I never see you again." He turned and walked rapidly out of the restaurant.

Andrew jumped up to run after him. "Wait!"

Mario pulled him back. "Let him go! We don't want him around."

"He should come with us," Andrew replied. "If we find the Skymaze now, he should be with us."

"Nah, he'll only mess things up even more. Come

on, let's go. We've wasted enough time already."

"Did you know this place was haunted?" Mario remarked as they climbed the concrete stairs to the top level of the car park.

"Yeah, sure," Andrew retorted. "By dead cars! Abandoned by their owners and left here to rust."

"No, seriously. Haunted by ghosts. A lot of kids come here to kill themselves. They jump off the top. And my brother, Frank, had a friend who owned a record shop on the ground floor. One night when he was locking up he saw evil spirits trying to get people to do themselves in."

"There's no such thing as ghosts or evil spirits," Andrew said scornfully, but he couldn't help being aware that the car park had a curious feeling to it that made him feel shivery and depressed, as though he was coming down with the flu. He kept thinking he could hear footsteps on the stairs behind them, but when he stopped to listen, they stopped too. He glanced sideways at Mario. He looked the same as he usually did, thin and white-faced, his shoulders hunched inside the black jacket, his hands shoved deep in the pockets, but his habitual air of loneliness seemed more marked.

"What are we doing here, anyway?" Mario asked as they reached the top level. It was almost empty of cars, and through the bars that had been installed to prevent people throwing themselves off, they could see the cranes, neon signs, and high-rise buildings that made up the city skyline, blurred and softened by the afternoon spring sunshine.

"We're looking for the Skymaze," Andrew said distractedly. He was disappointed to see nothing there that wasn't supposed to be there. He realised he had been hoping they would find the Skymaze activated and present, and be able to walk straight into it. But it wasn't going to be that easy. "How the heck are we going to find it?" he went on. "It could be anywhere! And will we just see it, or is there something we've got to do?"

Mario hitched himself up on to the sill overlooking the street and lit a cigarette. He passed the packet to Andrew, who took one, and then changed his mind and put it back again.

"I don't really like it," he explained, almost apologetically.

"Doesn't bother me if you like it or not," Mario replied. He blew the smoke out in a cloud, and watched it float away through the bars. "Long way down, isn't it! Can you imagine jumping off?"

Andrew shivered. It felt as if there was someone watching them, keeping an eye on them. He wondered fleetingly if Paul really had gone, or if he had followed them. He scanned the deserted car park quickly and then looked over the edge and tried to imagine how it would feel to fall that far.

"Have you ever wanted to?" he asked Mario.

"Now and again. Not recently. But it's always there, isn't it? I reckon it's a sort of fail-safe. If it all gets too tough, you can always opt out. But I don't intend to yet!" He grinned sideways at Andrew and winked. "Too many things to have a shot at first."

Both boys were silent for a few moments as they thought about life and death, and all the things there were to experience in between. The future hung before them, complex, alarming and enticing.

"But how are we going to get into it?" Andrew demanded impatiently.

Mario stopped contemplating the future and returned rather reluctantly to the present. He dropped his cigarette through the bars and watched it fall to the pavement below. "You know, this would be an ace place to drop light bulbs from," he said conversationally.

"It's a tempting idea," Andrew replied, "but we haven't got time for games now. Come on, use that under-employed brain of yours."

"I am," Mario assured him. "It's just that I think better when I'm thinking about something else. That's what's wrong with school—I can never think about things properly when I'm forced to think only about *them*. I've been thinking about it all the time—underneath."

"And what have you come up with?"

"This!" Mario dropped lightly from the sill, and in the same swift movement pulled something out of his pocket. Andrew gave a gasp of amazement when he saw it was a small, thin-bladed but all the same extremely sharp looking knife.

"Start praying," Mario hissed, advancing towards him in a menacing manner.

"Very funny," Andrew said sarcastically. "Stop mucking around. Don't you realise this could be life or death for Ben and Elly?"

"It's going to be life or death for you," Mario snarled back. "Probably death!"

"Oh migosh, he's gone bananas!" Andrew thought in panic. He backed away slowly, keeping his eyes on the knife. "It's all right, Mars," he said soothingly. "I'm your friend. I won't do anything to hurt you. Put the knife away."

"Hai!" Mario leaped and feinted towards him. Andrew jumped rapidly backwards. His heart was thumping, he felt hot and cold all over, and he could feel sweat starting to form under his collar. The

108

thought flashed through his mind that Mario had been taken over by one of the evil spirits he had been talking about earlier. He looked wildly round the car park. It was deserted. Whoever had been watching them before was definitely not there now. He opened his mouth to shout for help, but his voice had mysteriously disappeared. Mario stabbed towards him. It didn't seem possible that he could miss, he was so close, but he did. As he drew back to lunge again, Andrew did the only thing possible. He turned and ran.

He pelted for his life down the spiral to the next level, and was making for the door to the stairs, but Mario ran faster across the empty spaces and blocked his exit. Andrew dodged back, tore in the other direction, and found that he was ascending again, past where they had stood before, and up to the roof level.

"This is no good," he thought between agonising breaths. "This is a dead end."

To add to his panic, he thought he was going to faint, for around him darkness was falling. "I've had it!" he gasped in desperation. But to his surprise he did not fall and the darkness did not overwhelm him. Instead, it began to clear a little, and out of the corner of his eye he saw a shimmering. For a second he thought it was a spirit, and his heart stopped. Then, with a curious mixture of terror and relief, he leaped towards it, up into the air. For a moment he was suspended above the city. He felt the shimmer thicken and become real. All around him stars were appearing. Struggling and swaying, he pulled himself through the sky and sank down, panting and exhausted, in the first stage of Skymaze.

Despite his exhaustion, he stayed down only for a moment, as long as it took to realise that Mario was coming after him. He started to climb the ladder, his brain whirling. They had done it, they had found the Skymaze, but what use was it if he was fleeing through it himself? He could never hope to find Ben and Elaine on his own, and what about the Pale Guardians? Who or what were they, and what was he going to do about them? "Don't go crazy, Mars," he begged silently. "I need you!"

Through the conflicting ideas that absorbed him as he climbed upwards, he heard someone calling his name.

"Andy! Wait!"

It didn't sound like a homicidal maniac. But wouldn't a homicidal maniac be cunning enough to disguise his voice? Andrew climbed on doggedly, but the voice pursued him. "Hang on! It's okay. I'm not after you!"

Andrew came to the top of the ladder and crouched on the edge. "I can push you off from here," he warned. "I've got my boots and I can fly, but you can't. So don't try anything!"

Mario's head appeared at the top. He was grinning. "It worked," he crowed. "I did it! Pretty nifty, hey?"

He sounded as mad as ever, but in a different way. Andrew edged away from him nervously. "What on earth got into you?"

"I told you, I think about things while I'm thinking about something else! Well, it suddenly came to me in a flash. You get into the Skymaze because you run into it. You've got to be running away from someone, or something. I couldn't explain it, because then you wouldn't have been really scared. So I just did it!"

Andrew breathed a sigh of relief. "I thought you'd gone psycho!"

"Good performance, wasn't it?" Mario agreed with pride. "I reckon I should be on TV. Gee, it was fun too! You should have seen your face."

110

"You might have told me," Andrew complained. Inside he was smarting a little that it was Mario, and not he, who had grasped the secret of how to enter the Skymaze. He realised that Mario acted entirely on impulse, and while the impulses often seemed crazy and dangerous, they sprang from an intuition of truth that had not occurred to anyone else.

"Got any more bright ideas?" he asked grudgingly.

"Yeah, quite a few. But I'll tell you about them as we go. We'd better not hang around here, because I've got a horrible feeling that creep Paul can get in here after us. Now he's played the game, he'll know what to look for, and what to do once he's inside."

"You think he was following us in the car park?"

"Someone was," Mario replied grimly.

Andrew shivered. The idea that Paul might be pursuing them gave to the Skymaze a dimension of terror it had not had before.

"Is Paul one of the Pale Guardians?"

"That's what we have to find out. Let's get climbing!"

CHAPTER EIGHT

They began to work their way through the maze, as
alert and aware as a pair of cats. Nothing seemed to
have changed physically, but Andrew was conscious of
a subtle difference in the atmosphere. He was finding
the maze more fascinating and beautiful than ever, and
at the same time more alarming.

"It grows on you, doesn't it?" Mario muttered,
echoing his thoughts.

"Do you think that's good or bad?"

"I've got a feeling it's bad," Mario admitted. Then
he laughed. "But that's good. Makes it more exciting."

Andrew had an idea. "We're going to know if Ben's
in here or not, at least. If he is, we've got unlimited
time, and if he's not, the game's going to come to an
end pretty soon."

Mario nodded as he dodged an unidentified flying
object that whirled silently between them. They both
gazed after it, and then looked at each other and tried
to laugh.

"What *was* that?" Andrew asked.

"It was one of those missiles you always get here—it
just looked really gross for a moment." Mario had gone
paler than ever, but it was hard to tell if it was from fear

or excitement, and he shuddered before he went on, "We'd better make a plan in case we get separated. We don't want to run out of lives. When you're down to your last life, you just stay on the cliff, okay? Then we can go out together."

"Okay," Andrew agreed. He didn't like to ask what they would do if they hadn't found Ben and Elaine by then.

"We can always come back again," Mario said, as if he knew what Andrew was thinking. "But if we've lost all our lives, we'll be trapped too, and then who's going to rescue us?"

"Don't talk about that!" Andrew said with a shiver. He had a horrible feeling that for all its beauty and fascination the Skymaze had become deadly too.

They continued climbing and soon branched off on a new spiral they did not remember exploring before. After several bewildering twists and turns they came to a deep chasm that cut across the path.

"We can get across that," Mario said. It looked like an easy jump, but when they leaped, they realised that the narrowness of the gap was an illusion. The other side was much further away than it appeared. Andrew made it easily, thanks to the flying boots, but Mario fell through seemingly endless space, blacked out momentarily, and found himself back at the start of the game, on the cliff top, alone.

He took a deep breath while he wondered what to do next. The fall had been both terrifying and strangely exhilarating. It was a moment of complete surrender, when you realised you had to lose a life and there was nothing you could do about it. It combined fear of the darkness with trust that it would only be momentary. The feeling was quite unlike the despair that had

113

overtaken him when he had been shot in the game of Space Demons. That still gave him nightmares when he recalled it.

"But I always know I have another life to go," he thought. "I don't know what it would be like to die for the third time. Suppose that's like in Space Demons? Suppose then you get trapped forever?"

He was uncomfortably aware that no one else knew the secret of the Skymaze. They could disappear forever, and no one would ever know . . .

The atmosphere seemed more tense, and the background noise of the Skymaze, a sort of steely humming like high wires in the wind, more sinister.

Mario gave himself a shake. "I must get back in it," he thought. "There's no point going the way we just went, I'll never get across that gap." He looked rather disgustedly at the elixir of healing, hanging in its humble brown flask round his neck.

"Wish I'd had the boots," he thought. "It's typical that Hayford gets the best thing. I don't suppose this gunk is good for anything!" Feeling vaguely sorry for himself, he set out in the direction of the flowers.

Andrew was far away on a distant arm of the maze. When he saw Mario fall, he had hesitated between going back and going on alone. He decided to go on, feeling that with the flying boots he could go further and higher. "Mars can look after himself," he thought. "It'll be more useful if I go on. That way we can cover more of the maze." He also had a little half-hidden desire, which he could not quite admit to himself, to be the one to find the others first, to be the hero. "Typical of Ben," he thought rather scathingly, "to get himself stuck in here. But I'm going to rescue him. And Elaine!" Especially Elaine, the same half-hidden thought tried to suggest. The idea of rescuing Elaine made him feel so elated that he over-confidently tried to jump over some little cloud-like objects that were hovering across the path.

As he jumped he looked down, and for a split second he saw in them something so ugly and fearful that he cried out in horror and involuntarily closed his eyes. His foot brushed against one of the clouds, there was a flash of blue light, a noise like a chain saw, and he felt himself plunge into darkness and out of it again on to the cliff top.

There was no sign of Mario. Andrew swore excitedly to himself, half shocked and half exhilarated by his sudden death and resurrection. "What on earth was that dreadful-looking thing?" he wondered. "I don't remember seeing anything like that before." Then he thought, "Gee, only two lives to go. I'd better be a bit more careful!"

Mario was trying to be careful too. The knowledge that he was on his last chance was making him, usually the most reckless and impulsive of people, cautious. He was making his way carefully across a grey-and-silver walkway, suspended dizzyingly above a sheer drop on either side, when he realised to his despair that the walkway behind him was crumbling. He speeded up, but now the very boards under his feet disappeared as he touched them, and as they crumbled he had a glimpse of something horrific in their place, something he had only ever encountered in half-remembered nightmares. He flung himself forward desperately, but he could not save himself. Again there was the fall, the darkness, the sudden shock of reawakening; but this time there came with it the grim realisation that he had failed. The Skymaze hung before him, tantalising and mysterious, but he did not dare go into it.

For a while he lay face down on the cliff, waiting for Andrew, but the minutes passed and Andrew did not appear. Mario began to feel bored, then lonely, then uneasy. He sat up and drummed his fingers restlessly on his knees. He could not decide what to do. Why didn't Andrew come back to the cliff? Was it that he hadn't lost any lives? That seemed unlikely; he wasn't that good a player, despite the winged boots. Could he have lost all his lives? It was a horrible thought, but also quite unlikely. "He's a cautious sort of dude," Mario thought. "He would never have risked going back in with only one life left. Perhaps he came back to the cliff and left the game. Perhaps that's what I ought to do now."

For a long time he kept thinking that that was what he would do. He would get to his feet and walk back down the dark tunnel to . . . where had they been before? It seemed a lifetime ago. Yes, that's right, the car park. He grinned when he thought of Andrew's face as he had chased him through the cars, and felt a flash of pleasure that it had been he who had solved the puzzle of how to get into the Skymaze.

"I can trust myself," he thought. "If I do what feels right, it usually is the right thing to do. So what feels right now?"

Sitting on the cliff doing nothing didn't feel right, nor did walking out of the Skymaze altogether. The only thing that felt right was going back up!

Mario shook his head. "Crazy," he muttered, but he could feel himself starting to grin. He remembered what he had said to Andrew as they had gazed down from the top level of the car park. There was so much to experience, so much to live for, but right now he didn't care. The only thing that mattered was to return to the Skymaze. He jumped to his feet.

"Left hand, right hand?" he shouted aloud, and heard his words echo silkily back like the sound of the sea in a shell.

. . . Right hand . . .

"Right hand it is," he said, and started to scale the ladder.

But once he was up in the maze, his confidence started to drain away. Every object that came against him, every hazard he had to negotiate, seemed loaded with something unspeakable that got under his defences and made his skin crawl. His heart was thudding uncomfortably. Skymaze was no longer a game. It was no longer fun. The new level was filled with fear. He felt as though the Skymaze knew him, and knew all his hidden fears, and was now turning them against him.

He made his way painfully through the maze, no longer taking risks, but working out each level with exquisite care. He still needed his excellent reflexes and his boldness, but he added to these an element of prudence that was normally never part of his character. The further he went, the more he felt a sense of power returning to him.

"I can do it!" he thought grimly. "It's not really any more difficult than it was before. It's just trying to make me think it is. You just have to pretend the fear isn't there."

As he climbed higher than he had ever been before, it was as if he had forgotten what he was doing and why he was there. He no longer remembered that he and Andrew had come into the maze to find Ben and Elaine. He no longer even remembered that he did not know what had happened to Andrew. The only thing that seemed to matter now was to get to the centre of the maze, to explore it and discover all its secrets. He felt it belonged to him, it was his alone, and he alone would master it. And when he knew it entirely, he would know and master himself also. So when he came into another level of the maze and saw a pale, unconscious figure trapped against the wall, held there by bone-white hands that protruded from the shimmering surface, he stood and stared at it for some time before he realised who it was.

"Andy?" he said wonderingly.

The figure did not respond in any way. The hands did not move, nor did they show any sign of releasing their grip. Mario looked around apprehensively. He felt as if he was being watched, but there was no one there—just the hands sticking out in a revolting fashion from the wall. He found himself thinking suddenly of Paul. Were these white hands the work of the Pale Guardians?

He did not dare touch them. He did not dare move. He had no idea what move Andrew had made to fall captive to them. It could have been anything! And he could do that very same thing at any moment, and be trapped in the same way. For many minutes he stood petrified; his brain felt like a rock, incapable of thought or emotion.

Finally his gaze fell on the winged boots. "So they don't save you," he found himself thinking, with uncharacteristic sorrow. He remembered how he had been envious of the boots, how they had seemed to be one more example of all the unfair advantages Andrew had over him. Now, deep in the Skymaze, the tables had been turned, the scales balanced. Andrew had lost, and he, Mario, was, if not exactly the winner, the survivor.

He should have been glad, but he wasn't. He found himself thinking instead that Andrew was the closest thing to a mate he had ever had. He felt desperately sad and alone.

Not daring to move, he stood in the one spot and tried to think what to do next. "It's a game," he reminded himself. "Therefore we can get through it. There must be something I can do . . . or I've got . . . that gets us through this stage. I must be able to help him."

Then he remembered the elixir of healing. "Of course," he breathed in relief. "It's one of the objects to help us through the game; this must be the place to use it." He lifted the flask, and, trembling and slow, crept towards the unconscious boy. The white hands did not move, and nothing reached out to grab him, but as he rounded the curve he could see beyond, and his hair stood on end in fright.

Further along from where the hands held Andrew tight in their grip, he could see two other limp figures—Ben and Elaine. Their eyes were closed and their faces as white as the hands that clutched them. It was a horrible sight, like being in a room full of the ghosts of people who had been your friends, and it was all Mario could do to prevent himself from turning and running as fast as he could away from the terror and out of the Skymaze.

Possibly anyone else would have done. But Mario could not bear the thought of running away from anything. His courage had brought him through his own fears to this point. He was not going to back off now. He took another step towards Andrew, and then another, until he was close enough to touch him.

"I wonder what I do with it," he thought uncomfortably. He couldn't help feeling like an idiot as he took the top off the flask and poured a little of the elixir on to his hand, and he couldn't help wishing he had something more like a weapon. He thought with regret of the gun from Space Demons. That had made him feel like a hero, like someone powerful. Dabbling around with this peculiar stuff that looked like after-shave (and smelled a bit like after-shave too) made him feel awkward and silly.

In his awkwardness his hand slipped, and a drop of the clear liquid splashed down on to one of the hands that held Andrew in its relentless grasp. A shudder ran down the arm, and the hand dropped. For a moment it floated lifelessly from the wall, like a piece of slime or a dead fish, and then it began to wither and shrivel.

Mario didn't know whether to be delighted or disgusted. Feeling slightly nauseated, he splashed a drop on to the other hand, and caught Andrew's slumped figure as the second arm shrivelled and disappeared. Then, supporting Andrew with one hand, he poured a little of the elixir on to the top of his head.

Andrew gave a long-drawn-out shudder that convulsed his body from head to foot, and opened his eyes.

"Gee," he said weakly, "am I glad to see you!"

For a couple of moments they stood clutching each other. Then Andrew straightened up with an effort.

"Bring that stuff," he said, in a ghost of his usual voice. "Let's see if it works on the others."

"What happened?" Mario said softly, as they crept with infinite care towards the two pale figures in the grasp of the ghastly hands.

"I just came on Ben and Elaine," Andrew said, with another shudder. "I couldn't get them away from those . . . those hands, and when I turned round to go back, they grabbed me too! They come out of the walls," he added, looking round nervously and trying to hide his fear. Then he gave up trying and admitted, "I've never been so frightened in my life!"

"What sets them off?" Mario said, whispering as if he was afraid the hands could actually hear him.

"Paul must have set them off, by choosing the gun. These must be the Pale Guardians."

"Did you see Paul anywhere?"

"No, but I saw all sorts of really gross things—and then, when you look at them, they aren't really there. The whole game's changed. He's ruined it."

"But something must have made them start guarding. Why here? Why now? Why not on any of the other stages we've been through this time?"

"Wake the others up," Andrew said urgently. "See what they know."

They were now close enough to the silent, slumped figures of Elaine and Ben to reach out and touch them. Ben was slightly closer to them, his head thrown back and his legs drawn up, as though he had made one last desperate leap before being trapped. Beyond him Elaine's copper hair glowed brightly, contrasting strangely with the monochromatic world of the Skymaze. Her head drooped forwards, showing the nape of her neck, making her look fragile and defenceless.

Mario carefully poured the elixir on to the hands that imprisoned Ben. They watched in revulsion as the pale limbs twitched, shrivelled and disappeared. Then Andrew caught and held Ben, and Mario let a few drops of liquid fall on his upturned face.

Ben shivered, opened his eyes, shivered again, and sneezed violently

"Look after him for a moment," Mario said to

121

Andrew. "I'll get Elaine." The thought flashed through his mind that if he was unable to revive her, he would find the nearest cliff and leap howling off the edge. But he didn't have to. She shivered like Ben, and came to, her eyes blank for a few seconds, until she looked at him and focused on his face. Then she threw her arms round his neck and hugged him.

"Don't anyone move!" Ben said as soon as he could talk. His voice was weak, but there was no mistaking the urgency in it.

"Why?" Mario turned, about to step back towards Ben and Andrew, but froze to the spot when Ben shrieked, "Don't come back!"

"That's what we did," Elaine added swiftly. "We started to go back, and that's when those revolting things grabbed us!"

"You mean we can't retrace our steps?" Andrew said incredulously. "Then how are we going to get out?"

The same thought had occurred to them all simultaneously. Nobody said anything. Nobody moved.

"What happens if you go forwards?" Andrew said at last.

"I just did that," Mario reminded him. "That's no problem."

"So that's what the Guardians do," Andrew said slowly. "They mean you can only go on. So, that's what we've got to do. We've got to go on and solve it."

"*If* it can be solved," Ben said.

"Of course it can be solved! It's a game—it's got to be able to be played. It's got to have rules."

"It's all very well having rules, when it knows them and we don't!" Mario remarked.

Elaine started to speak, rather hesitantly, since what she was going to say was not exactly very helpful to them right then. "I have the feeling there's something else we need. It's something I feel as if I'm missing."

"She never got to choose anything from the grotto," Ben explained. "She really needs to play the game on the computer and choose her object, whatever it is."

Mario and Andrew looked at each other. "What was it Paul said?" Andrew demanded.

"'A true sense of direction'," Mario replied slowly. "That's what we need all right! But first we've got to get out!"

"Not much of a choice, is it?" Ben said, trying to sound light-hearted about it. "We go on, we can't find the way; we go back, we get caught by the Guardians. Anyone got any bright ideas?"

"We'd better try and end the game," Andrew said. "You could do what you did last time—get yourself killed, and then walk out."

"Can you still do that, now the Guardians have been activated?" Mario questioned. "What happens if they operate down there at that level too?"

"You go down with him, and use the last of the elixir to get you both through," Andrew suggested.

Mario was silent for a moment, and then he admitted, "I've got no lives left!"

They all stared at him without saying anything, as the implications of what he had said sank in.

Andrew spoke first. "You mean, you came after us after you'd lost two lives?"

Mario nodded, starting to feel extremely embarrassed by the way they were looking at him. "Only because I didn't want to stay down there on my own."

Andrew shook his head in unwilling admiration. "You must be crazy!"

"Just as well he is!" Ben exclaimed. "What would we have done if he wasn't!"

"Don't go on about it," Mario said. He sounded off-

123

hand, but inside he felt better than he could ever remember feeling in his life. These people were his friends! He had rescued them. They were grateful to him. They admired him. He no longer cared if they got to the end of the Skymaze or not! It seemed to him nothing could make him feel better than he did right now.

"Still, that doesn't help us now," Andrew was saying apprehensively. "Mario, you can't try going down with Ben. In fact, you'd better not risk going anywhere." He frowned as he tried to puzzle out the rules of the game as they knew them so far. He was just coming to the decision that the only thing they could do was to send Ben back to the beginning to try and end the game, when Elaine said suddenly, "I can hear something!"

They all turned towards the end of the tunnel where they had been held by the hands of the Guardians. There was a shadow on the silvery wall. Someone was standing just beyond the curve.

Mario hissed in Andrew's ear, "It must be Paul!"

That was all there was time to say. In the instant between recognising Paul, and realising he was not going to be friendly, they could do nothing but stand frozen to the spot.

Paul lifted the gun and let it fire. They had time to feel one moment of intense sorrow for the Skymaze, which had been turned into something lethal, followed by total panic as they realised what this meant for Mario, and then everything went black.

Elaine, Ben and Andrew found themselves back on the cliff top. The Skymaze still soared above them, and behind them, at the end of the dark tunnel, they caught a dim glimpse of the car park. Frantic, they looked around, and then Elaine grabbed Andrew's arm and screamed at him, "Where is he? Where's Mars?"

"I don't know," he shouted back, feeling sick. "How am I supposed to know? I don't know what happens if you lose all three lives."

"Let's get out of here," Ben said quietly. "We can't go back looking for him now."

"But we can't just go out, not knowing what's happened to him. What if he's stuck inside the Skymaze somewhere? We've got to go back for him!"

"Ben's right," Andrew said sadly. "We've got to end this game now. All the odds are against us, we're running out of lives, we can't retrace our steps because of the Guardians, and we've got that maniac Paul running around after us with the gun. I say we try to get out now, then we play the game on the computer and start again."

Elaine looked in confusion towards the real world at the end of the tunnel. "What about those vile hands? Are they going to grab us down here?"

"I reckon not," Andrew said slowly. "I think this is a sort of neutral ground. The game doesn't start properly until you get above the cliff. I think we'd be safe to go out from here."

Nobody moved for a moment. The choices before them all seemed too desperate and difficult. In the end Ben said, "You stay here. Once I'm out, the game will end. But if anything gets me, you'll have to go back in and work out what to do from the inside."

"I'm on my last life now," Andrew couldn't help saying.

"Then I just hope I get out!" Ben replied.

The first step was the worst. In his mind's eye he could imagine taking the step, and feeling again the dread he had felt when the hands had reached out from the walls

125

and clutched him. Icy cold they were, sucking all the warmth and life from him until he had collapsed unconscious in their grasp. Just the thought of them now made him nearly faint with fear. He took the first step, and nothing happened, and then the second, and the third, and then his confidence slowly returned as he realised he was going to make it.

The stars were fading; the cliff top was changing, giving way to concrete and metal. The light changed from the unearthly gleam of the Skymaze to the orange glow of sunset over the city. Ben blinked his eyes hard. He wasn't sure if he was crying or if his eyes were watering because he was blinded by the evening sun pouring in through the openings in the car park.

His legs gave way and he sat down heavily on the ground. He found he was staring intently at a patch of oil on the concrete. It struck him as vaguely interesting. His mind refused to think about anything else.

He was still staring at it several minutes later when the game ended. Unseen by anyone, the Skymaze faded. There was a brief flash in the sky that might have been lightning, and Andrew and Elaine found themselves slumped next to Ben on the top level of the car park. Elaine had tears pouring down her face, and Andrew buried his head in his arms. They all felt terrible—exhausted, grief-stricken and guilty. They did not notice Paul Freeman, flexing the hand that had held the gun, cross the roof with a look of amazed triumph on his face, and disappear swiftly down the stairs. They heard only dimly the frantic shrilling of a siren as an ambulance tore down the street six storeys below.

"Come on," Andrew said at last. He seemed to be recovering more quickly than the other two. "We can't sit here all night. Everyone's worried sick about you two already. We've got to get home."

"Yeah, you're right," Ben said, struggling weakly to his feet. "Only problem is, we're never going to make it!" He swayed against a pillar, and sank down again. "I honestly don't think I can walk!"

"What about you, Elly?"

Elaine didn't answer. She just shook her head at Andrew and the tears went on coursing silently down her cheeks.

"I think I'd better go and phone home," Andrew said. "I'll tell them where we are and they'll come and get us."

There was an orange phone on the ground level of the car park. When Andrew came out of the lift, feeling in the pocket of his jeans to see if he had the right change, he was surprised to see quite a crowd standing round the car park entrance. He needed a ten cent piece for the phone and he asked a young woman near him if she had one. While she was fumbling in her handbag, he couldn't stop himself asking, "What happened? What's everyone staring at?"

Her eyes gleaming, she said with relish, "A kid jumped off the roof. The ambulance just came and took him to hospital!"

Andrew heard his own voice say, "Was he dead?"

"I reckon! He fell six storeys! Here you go, mate, here's ten cents."

"Thanks," Andrew said mechanically. Inside he was saying over and over to himself, "Mario, oh God, Mario, oh God, don't let him be dead!"

Then he went to the phone and dialled his own number. It rang three times before his stepfather answered it, saying in his friendly, professional voice, "Keith Freeman speaking!"

Andrew had never been so pleased to hear him

before. "Keith," he said, hearing his voice start to break as he said it, "Keith, it's me. I've found Ben and Elaine. Can you please come and get us?"

CHAPTER NINE

"Well, he's alive," Keith said to Andrew as he slid back into the front seat of the Lancia outside the Children's Hospital.

Andrew had been watching the pattern of the street lights on the giant Moreton Bay fig trees in the park opposite and trying not to think about anything. Now he turned eagerly to Keith and said, "You mean, he's going to be all right?"

"It's a bit early to say that. He's still unconscious, but he's breathing quite normally, and there's no sign of internal injuries. Bloody lucky. Something must have broken his fall. Did you see it? What actually happened?"

"We weren't there," Andrew said. "We were somewhere else."

"But what in heaven's name were you all doing?"

"We were playing a sort of game," Andrew said rather weakly. He had been dreading the moment when the questions started. Keith had not said very much to any of them so far. He had taken Ben and Elaine home, spoken briefly to Ben's parents and the Fields, and then driven to the hospital to find out what had happened to Mario. Now he studied Andrew's face as he started the car, but it was only a couple of minutes before they were home, and he did not say more than, "We'll talk about it later."

As soon as Andrew stepped into the hall he saw Paul, who was sitting half-way up the stairs as though he had been waiting for them. Neither of the boys spoke, but Paul gave Andrew a look that Andrew could not quite decipher. He was too exhausted and distraught, and Keith and Marjorie were distracting him by suggesting that he should have something to eat, a bath, a hot drink and go to bed. Since Andrew couldn't think of anything else to do—in fact, he could hardly think at all—this seemed like a good idea. He let his mother fuss over him and tuck him up in bed, and he lay there drinking hot Milo and feeling rather comfortably like a seven-year-old, except that every now and then he remembered what had happened and a wave of pure panic swept over him, making him tremble and spill the Milo on his pillow.

He turned the pillow over, dry side up, and his fingers felt the hard edge of the Skymaze disc. He took it out and looked at it, remembering how he had slipped it inside the pillow to hide it after coming back from Ben's the weekend before. It was only a week ago, but it seemed like an eternity. Then he thought in despair of Paul taking it and playing it. When he tried to think of what to do next he felt numb and shaky. He thought of Mario, lying unconscious in hospital. "That could have been me," he said to himself. "It could have been any one of us. And it still could be," his mind added.

He fell asleep holding the disc, and dreamed of the Skymaze calling out to him. He woke several times in the night, in the grip of a terrifying sense of urgency, and when he slept for the last time before morning, in

130

his dream the voice calling out to him was Mario's.

"No change," Keith reported after a quick visit into the hospital on Sunday morning. "His parents have been in there all night. His mother is absolutely beside herself." He gave Andrew a searching look, and went on, "You don't think he meant to fall in some way?"

"No, he didn't," Andrew replied impatiently. He was trying to concentrate on what they should be doing next, and he very much wanted to talk to Ben about it. He couldn't explain to Keith what had happened without getting involved in some outrageous lies, and if he was going to have to tell lies he wanted to be sure Ben and Elaine were telling the same ones.

"The charge sister thinks he might have done. From what she's gathered from Mario's mother, they've had a lot of problems with him."

"Yeah, well, maybe that's their fault," Andrew replied.

"Did he ever talk about taking his own life?"

"Not really."

"But he did in some way?"

Keith could be very insistent, Andrew thought. He never gave up when he was on the track of something. "He said he used to think about it, but he didn't any more," he tried to explain. "But that had nothing to do with what happened. He didn't jump on purpose. He . . . he must have just fallen . . ."

What had happened, really? He hadn't stopped asking himself that all morning. The Skymaze had thrown Mario out because he had lost all his lives. It had thrown him out from the great height they had been on, back into the real world. But the fall hadn't killed him, so perhaps the game had also been protecting him in some way. Andrew frowned as he

131

tried to puzzle it all out.

Keith sighed. "Kids do some funny things when they're thirteen and fourteen. It's a shame we have no real rites of passage. It would do you all good to be packed off to the boys' house and put through initiation ceremonies."

Andrew didn't know what he was talking about now, but he found he was resenting the fatherly tone. "Actually, I don't think it's any of your business," he said insolently, hoping to put an end to the whole conversation.

Keith surprised him by reacting very strongly to this. "It is my business," he said loudly. "It is my business because I happen to care about you and your friends, and I care about what happens to you."

"I don't see why," Andrew retorted. "You're not my father." He was aware that this hit home, and that Keith was making quite an effort to control himself. It seemed a good moment to escape. "I think I'll go over to Ben's," he said, getting up and making for the door.

"I'm afraid that's out of the question," Keith replied, also getting up swiftly. He didn't actually stop Andrew going through the door, but there was every indication he was quite prepared to. "We all feel it would be better if you and Ben and the girl didn't see each other for a little while."

"Is this some kind of punishment?" Andrew demanded indignantly.

"You can call it that if you like. I prefer to call it a precaution. Ben's parents, and your mother and I, feel you've all had a bit too much freedom. You've been allowed to do things on your own, and you've shown that you can't handle it. With pretty disastrous consequences, I might add. So we've all decided you're to stay close to home for a while, and we're going to be

132

keeping a bit more of an eye on you."

Andrew swore angrily. "What about Paul? Does he have to stay close to home too?"

Keith sounded just as angry. "Don't try and shift the blame on to Paul, Andrew! He had nothing to do with this particular escapade. He says he left you at the restaurant."

"Then he's lying! It was all his fault," Andrew said furiously. "If he hadn't meddled with stuff that belongs to me, it wouldn't have all gone wrong!"

"I think it's time you looked at this childish jealousy of yours, and did something about it! You and Paul are in the same family, like it or not, and I am not going to let you spoil the happiness we could have! You might think about your mother. You are making her absolutely miserable."

"Oh, it's no use talking to you," Andrew said bitterly. "You don't understand anything!"

"I think you need to spend some time on your own to cool off, Andy," Keith said, making a huge effort to regain his professional tone, which he had lost completely during the course of the argument.

"Suits me fine," Andrew flung back. To his satisfaction he managed to bang three doors hard on his way to his bedroom.

The satisfaction did not last long, however. Once he was in his room, it hit him all too strongly how helpless he was. And to make things worse, he kept having an odd sensation—like a physical memory of the white hands on his skin. It made him shudder all over, and it made him shy away from the thought of the Skymaze. He felt he would give anything not to have to play the game again. Then he thought of Mario's voice, calling out to him.

133

"I can't give up," he told himself. He set himself the task of going doggedly over the different rules of the game in his mind. He remembered what Elaine had said back in the Skymaze, just before the disaster, something about her needing to play and choose an object. That made sense, but how was he going to get her to play the game if they weren't allowed to see each other? For the hundredth time he wished he was at Fernleigh High with Ben and Elaine, and not on the other side of the city. He was lying on his bed staring at the cornices beneath the ceiling, knowing that there was no alternative but to play on, when there was a very quiet knock at his door, and Paul's voice whispered, "Andrew, let me in!"

"What do you want?" Andrew returned, not bothering to get off the bed. He and Paul had not said a word to each other about Skymaze, but Andrew had not forgotten the look they had exchanged the night before. He thought about it now. Had it been threatening or had it been pleading? It was hard to say—a mixture of the two, perhaps, which was why it had been so difficult to read.

Paul's voice now sounded equally ambiguous. "Don't shout, I don't want anyone to hear. Let me in, I've got to talk to you."

"Yeah, I can think of one or two things to say to you too," Andrew snorted, getting up and opening the door a fraction.

Paul came hurriedly into the room, and grabbed Andrew urgently by the shoulders. "You've got to help me!"

"Don't touch me!" Andrew yelled. He twisted out of Paul's grasp, the memory of the hands becoming suddenly horrifyingly real.

"Keep your voice down," Paul hissed. "If Dad hears

us he'll crack up. You're supposed to be having 'time out'. That means no one's meant to be talking to you."

"That might be how I prefer it," Andrew said slowly, retreating out of Paul's reach and sitting down on the bed. Paul took this as an invitation to stay, and perched on the desk with his feet on the chair. There was a long moment of silence and then Andrew said grudgingly, "What did you want to talk about?" He still could not fathom if Paul had come as friend or enemy. Paul seemed friendly enough, far more friendly in fact than Andrew had ever known him, but every now and then something menacing surfaced in his voice and his eyes, and he looked at Andrew as though he wanted to kill him. Then he made a huge effort to control himself and the menace was hidden again, although his eyes still held something desperate and possessed in their depths.

Finally Paul said, "It's hard to talk about. It's like a terrible dream. I can't believe it really happened."

"It happened," Andrew said shortly. "You wouldn't listen to me when I tried to tell you. You took the gun when you shouldn't have. And then you shot us all!"

"I didn't know," Paul exclaimed. "I just thought you were being stupid and selfish. I didn't know that was what the gun did. The game was so fascinating. I wanted to play it with you. I didn't mean to shoot you all. It was the gun. The gun shot you."

"That's what guns do, you moron." Andrew couldn't resist the temptation to rub it in.

There was a flash of rage in Paul's eyes, and he spoke very rapidly. "Andrew, you've got to help me. It's worse than you think. It's got a hold on me. It won't let me go. It's going to make me do something terrible."

"What do you mean?"

"It keeps talking to me, inside my head. It says

135

things like, 'You are now the Guardian, you must protect the secret of the Skymaze.' It's trying to make me . . . you know, hurt you."

"Make you!" Andrew exclaimed. "You've been trying to hurt me ever since the first day I met you! What else is new?"

Paul gave him a look of pure hatred, and then groaned. "I might not have been very nice to you, I might have hassled you a bit, but I didn't want to kill you!"

Put like that, it sounded a little blunt. Andrew found he was staring at his stepbrother with his mouth open.

"I feel as if I'm going crazy," Paul exclaimed, jumping off the desk and pacing across the room and back. "You've got to do something. You've got to help me!"

"I'm not sure I know what to do," Andrew replied in confusion.

"You'd better think of something quickly." Paul sounded even more confused. He clutched his head in his hands. He seemed to be struggling to speak.

Andrew watched him in amazement. He couldn't help feeling sorry for him. "Hey," he said. "Hey, Paul. Calm down. I'll think of something. It's a game. It's got to be able to be played. We just have to work out the rules."

"You don't understand," Paul burst out. "I feel as if I'm being torn in two. Half of me wants to help you, and the other half wants to prevent you at all costs. That boy, your friend . . ." His voice choked away suddenly.

"Mario? What about him? What do you know about him?"

"Unless you solve the maze, he'll never wake up," Paul shouted, trying to get the whole sentence out

136

while he could. Then he went white. "I wasn't meant to tell you that," he said. "I didn't mean to tell you. I'm meant to be trying to stop you solving it. But if you don't solve it, he's going to be stuck like that forever— and so am I!"

"How do you know all this?"

"When I followed you into the game, the gun came into my hand," Paul said, still amazed at the memory. "It was really weird, it felt as if it was part of me. And then I could hear something talking to me inside my head, a funny kind of voice. At first it was nice—it said some really flattering things, like what a great games player I was, and what a terrific shot. And then it got a bit sinister, and it told me I belonged to it and I had to do what was needed. And then it told me all about Mario. The four of you who were in the game when I was following you make up one player, and the game and me make up the other. It's you against us. You've lost one life, so you've got three more to go." He looked up at Andrew in desperation. "And it keeps saying things like, 'The game has to be played to the bitter end!'."

"Don't panic," Andrew tried to reassure him. "We can do it. We can play it to the end. And we can win."

"Just don't ask me how right now," he added to himself.

Both boys were silent. Paul leaned back against the bookshelf, exhausted by his inner struggle. Andrew was thinking hard. Finally he said, "We'd better try playing the game again. Perhaps you can put the gun back. How long am I going to have this 'time out' or whatever it's called?"

"It all depends if you apologise or not. If you go down and act repentant you can probably get out now."

"I suppose it's worth it," Andrew said reluctantly.

137

"As long as nobody asks me what I'm really feeling."
He found he was feeling surprisingly sympathetic
towards Paul. "I don't know how you stood it for all
those years. No wonder you're a bit strange!"

For a moment the boys were united in contemplating
the quirky ways of adults. They did not say anything,
but they grinned shyly at each other.

"Well, come on, then!" Andrew said, getting up
from the bed. "Let's get it over with. But you go first.
I don't want you pushing me down the stairs because
you can't help yourself!"

Keith accepted Andrew's apology with delight and said
how glad he was the boys wanted to do something
together: certainly they could use the computer. But
playing the game was only frustrating. When they
played together, Paul could not prevent the Pale
Guardian image from shooting Andrew at every
opportunity; and when, playing on his own, he finally
made it to the grotto, he was not able to let go of the
gun. The computer informed them in its cool neutral
voice, *No second choice can be made. Only a new
player can activate the Skymaze. Guardians cannot be
released until the game is over.*

"That's rather what I suspected," Andrew said,
taking out the disc and switching off the computer.
"That just leaves Elaine. She's the only person left
who's played Space Demons, and who hasn't chosen
anything in Skymaze. We have to get the disc to her so
she can play."

"But what is Space Demons?" Paul asked curiously.

"That's another story!" Andrew replied. "I'll tell
you about it some time." He went on, thinking out
loud, "I don't think Elaine's got a computer at her
place, so she'll have to play at Ben's—and as soon as

138

possible. And then we all have to be together so we can get into the maze when it's activated."

"Where will it be?" he thought, "and how will we get in? What are we going to be running away from?" He looked up and caught Paul's eyes on him. Once again the look was a strange mixture of malevolence and helplessness. It made Andrew shiver.

"I could take the disc over," Paul suggested. "I haven't been grounded."

It sounded like a reasonable idea, yet Andrew hesitated. Suppose Paul threw the disc away, or destroyed it? He was hardly answerable for his own actions at the moment. There was no knowing what he might do.

"No, I think it might be safer in the post," he said slowly. "I'll post it after school tomorrow. But I'll phone Ben up now, and tell him what's happening and what he and Elaine have got to do. You go and stand guard and make sure no one's eavesdropping on me."

CHAPTER TEN

Another week began, and the first two days of it dragged by. Andrew, with considerable apprehension, committed Skymaze to the post, together with a rather incoherent letter in which he tried to explain to Ben all that Paul had told him about the game. In the meantime he tried to be as nice as he could to Paul to allay any possibly malicious intentions. But anxiety and impatience made it difficult, and by Tuesday evening he felt as if he was on the point of exploding, when Ben phoned with the welcome news that the game had arrived.

"But I don't know when we're going to get to play it," he told Andrew. "We aren't allowed to see each other all week."

"You'd better think of a way, quickly," Andrew replied impatiently. "And as soon as possible." He looked anxiously round the hallway to make sure no one was listening, and then whispered down the phone, "Can't you bludge school tomorrow?"

"That's not going to go down very well," Ben complained, also under his breath. "You don't know how tense things are over here. Everyone's watching me all the time. If I do one more crazy thing, I've

140

had it!"

"Well, if you don't, we've all had it!" Andrew replied as forcefully as he could in a whisper. "Didn't you read my letter? Elaine's got to play the game as soon as possible, and she's got to choose the true sense of direction. It looks like a compass as far as I can gather from Paul."

"Okay," Ben said. "We'll play it tomorrow—somehow. But then what? If we activate the maze, how are we going to get into it?"

"I've got a scheme for that," Andrew said. "It's a bit complicated, but you know how Keith is so keen on us all learning to be responsible and so on?"

"Yes, as a matter of fact I do know!" Ben replied with feeling. "I've heard about nothing else from Mum and Dad since Saturday. You'd think the sun shone out of his bum!"

"Well, your old man's into that sort of thing too, isn't he? Didn't you once tell me he was doing a counselling course?"

"Yup, he's still doing it."

"Sailing is a wonderful way to learn responsibility and co-operation, did you know that?"

"You're losing me!" Ben said.

"I'm going to suggest we all get together on Saturday for a family type outing, us and you and Elaine. Keith can take us all sailing, he always likes that. Then we'll all be together, at least."

"It's an idea," Ben conceded. Then he groaned, "Listen, I've got to go. Mum's yelling at me to get off the phone. I'll talk to you tomorrow."

Ben had planned to meet Elaine on the way to school, but when he spotted her at the pedestrian crossing, she was walking with John Ferrone. John's normally

141

cheerful face was pale, and there were dark shadows under his eyes.

"Any news?" Ben asked.

John shook his head. "Just the same. Mum came home last night. Frank went in to sit with Mars, just in case he woke up, so Mum could get some sleep, but she said she couldn't sleep anyway. I keep thinking, they always act like they don't care for him. Then something like this happens, and they care so much. What if he never wakes up and he never knows? I can't stop thinking about it. I wish I could tell him."

"Don't worry." Elaine gave his arm a squeeze. "At least he's still alive."

John sighed, but did not answer. Ben said, rather awkwardly, not wanting to upset him more, but desperate to speak to Elaine, "Johnny, do you mind if I talk to Elaine? I've got something I've got to tell her."

John still said nothing. He hunched his shoulders up inside his parka in a gesture that was just like Mario's, and walked slowly away from them.

"You didn't have to do that!" Elaine exclaimed in disgust. "Can't you see he's miserable enough already?"

"I know!" Ben replied. "But I've got to talk to you. We've got to get together and play the game today. We're going to have to bludge school and go to my place."

"Don't be crazy," Elaine said. "We're supposed to be being sensible this week. I'm in terrible trouble at . . ." She had been going to say "at home", but it wasn't feeling much like home at the moment. "At the Fields'," she finished lamely. "I'm on what they call 'last chance'. If I do anything else wrong, I can't do Shaz's show."

"They wouldn't stop you doing that? They can't!"

Ben knew how much it meant to Elaine to work with Shaz.

Elaine shrugged her shoulders. "I don't know. Auntie Jan said if I could keep out of trouble, she'd think about taking me in to the next rehearsal on Friday, but she'd stay there with me and watch. Imagine trying to do the sort of things we did last time with her looking on! It's going to be impossible. And all the others will laugh at me—having my foster mother along. I think she thinks I'm going to disappear if I'm not under her eye all the time. The only time I get away from her is at school."

"That's why we have to play the game during school."

"Can't we leave it for a little while?" She knew they couldn't, but she felt an enormous reluctance to get entangled in the Skymaze again.

"Everything's got rather dodgy all of a sudden," Ben said. "Andrew thinks that if we don't solve the maze, Mario won't ever come out of that coma or whatever he's in."

Elaine did not say anything for a few minutes. She swung her school bag viciously to and fro. Ben hopped out of the way. She seemed to be swearing under her breath, but he couldn't quite hear. "What's up?" he said rather nervously, hoping she wasn't going to lose her temper with him.

"I'm just furious," she snapped. "I'm furious about everything. It's all going wrong. I've *got* to be in the show. I'm *going* to be in it. I'm not doing anything else that's going to mess that up!" She tried not to think of John Ferrone slouching away from them earlier, looking suddenly so like his brother. And she tried not to think of the dreams that she too had been having, like Andrew, in which the Skymaze called out to her in Mario's voice. She knew, deep inside, that Ben was right, and they were going to have to play the game; but she didn't want to, and it made her very angry.

She stormed away from him as the siren went for the beginning of school, and he watched her go in despair. He spent the first two periods, double maths, biting his nails, completely oblivious to the finer points of trigonometry, but when he was walking to his next lesson Elaine waylaid him in the corridor .

"Okay," she hissed at him. "I'll do it. I'll meet you at your place after recess."

He nodded at her, speechless with relief. The first hurdle was over. He tried not to think of all the others that remained.

At recess Elaine walked purposefully out of the school gates, trying to look as though she was going somewhere perfectly legal and permissible like the dentist's, and made her way as inconspicuously as possible to the street where Ben lived. It wound rather steeply up the Hills face, and she was warm and out of breath by the time she came to the house. As Ben had promised, it looked deserted, and when she slipped quietly round to the back, he was waiting for her by the door.

"Did you have any problems?"

"Not so far," she replied shortly, pushing her fringe back up from her face.

Ben unlocked the door and they went stealthily into the silent house. It had an unfamiliar feel to it, as if it had not been expecting anyone and was mildly surprised to see them.

"I feel like a burglar," Elaine whispered.

"You don't have to whisper," he replied out loud, making her jump. "There's no one here. I'm just going to get the game from my room. You wait here."

He came back with it in his hand, and led Elaine through the house to his parents' study. He switched the computer on, inserted the disc, and boldly typed RUN SKYMAZE. Then they both watched the screen in tense anticipation. Elaine realised she was shivering. Now it was just a game, but she couldn't help remembering how much more than a game it had been before. There was a chill in the room that reminded her of the white hands. She looked nervously round as if they might suddenly appear here and grab her.

"Are you okay?" Ben asked her.

"Yeah, but let's get it over with as quickly as we can. It's giving me the creeps."

Ben drew a deep breath as the cliff top appeared on the screen. He had plugged in both joysticks, and he and Elaine took one each.

"That's weird!" Elaine exclaimed as she saw her own tiny image start to move around on the screen.

"Concentrate," Ben muttered. "We haven't got all day!"

They had been playing silently and painstakingly for about half an hour, and had still not found their way to the grotto, when to their horror they heard footsteps running along the side of the house. Elaine dropped the joystick and grabbed Ben's arm.

"Who's that?"

They heard the kitchen door open, and then there was silence, except for some intermittent tiny sounds that suggested someone was trying to creep noiselessly through the house.

Ben was biting his lip. The computer made a series of loud noises like a buzz saw as Elaine lost a life. They heard a rattle from the door and turned to see it open, centimetre by centimetre, to reveal Darren staring at them with a look of total disbelief on his face.

145

"What the hell are you two doing here?" he demanded belligerently. "I thought the house was being burgled when I found the kitchen door unlocked."

Ben made a noise of disgust. "What are *you* doing here? Why aren't you at school?"

"I've come back to do some studying, little brother. Have you forgotten I've got Matric next term? I haven't bludged school to play computer games! Just wait till Mum and Dad hear about this. I'd have thought you were in enough trouble already this week."

"Aw, come on, Darren, you don't have to tell them! Didn't you ever bludge school when you were thirteen?"

Darren replied to this plea with a non-committal snort. His attention was then caught by the computer game. A look of keen interest crossed his face and he approached the computer.

"Is this a new game? Where'd you get it?"

"Once a hacker, always a hacker," Ben thought to himself. "Andrew Hayford lent it to me," he said cautiously.

"Oh, that creep!" Darren had never been impressed by Andrew. He was, however, quite impressed by the game. "That's neat," he commented as he peered at the tiny figures, and looked from the screen to Elaine. "I've never seen that before. I wonder how they did it. What's this game called?"

"Skymaze," Ben replied reluctantly.

"Who's it put out by?"

"No one you've ever heard of. It comes from Japan."

"Fascinating," Darren murmured.

Ben could practically see Darren's fingers itching. "He's going to ask to play it;" he thought. "And how am I going to stop him?"

"Shove over," Darren ordered. "Let me have a shot."

"You can't," Ben said. "You can only play this game if you played the first game in the series."

"Huh?" Darren looked bewildered. "Who's to know?"

"The game knows," Ben started to explain, and then stopped. He couldn't explain the complexity of the two computer games to Darren, and even if he could, Darren would never believe him!

"You just mustn't," he said feebly.

"Bullshit! Shove over!"

Elaine was getting fed up with the two of them acting as if she wasn't there at all. "Didn't you get the message?" she said angrily. "You can't play this game. Why don't you get lost?"

Darren looked at her incredulously, and then turned back to the screen without saying anything. "Run the program again," he ordered Ben. "I'll give you a quick game."

"Don't do it!" Elaine said to Ben. "Don't let him push you around. Shove off," she told Darren. "We've told you, you can't play this game. So leave us alone."

"You're in no position to tell anyone to do anything," he replied. "Either I play the game now or I tell everyone what you and my brother get up to when you're meant to be at school. Which way do you want it?"

Ben swore under his breath.

"Now, now!" Darren said reprovingly. "You know Mum doesn't like bad language. I shall tell her what you called me."

"How did this happen?" Ben asked himself. "He's cornered me again." He could feel a futile rage rising inside him. He struggled to control it, trying to think clearly so he could work out what would be the least harmful course to take now.

147

"You really won't tell Mum and Dad we were here today?"

"Cross my heart!" Darren replied theatrically, giving Elaine a triumphant wink. She ignored it, scowling back at him.

"I know it's a risk," Ben was thinking, "but we've got to play the game now. We may never get another chance, and Elly's got to get the compass if we're ever going to solve the maze. If she can just get up to the grotto, that's all we need."

Hoping desperately he was doing the right thing, he said casually, "You can play with Elaine," and got up so Darren could take his place in front of the screen.

"You see," Elaine said coldly to Darren when the warning against playing Skymaze appeared. She was very angry with him, and rather disgusted with Ben for giving in to him. She was also full of mixed feelings about what they should have done. To be found out playing computer games at Ben's house when she was meant to be at school would put the lid once and for all on her hopes of being in Shaz Christie's show. She knew she had to play the game while she had the chance. But how she hated being intimidated by people like Darren!

He made her dislike him even more by saying mock-apologetically, "Sorry, oh, do please forgive me, mighty computer game," to which the computer made no reply.

Their two players appeared on the screen. Elaine's was the same tiny image of herself, but Darren's was a dark, menacing figure, black-hooded and cloaked. Ben gazed on it with a terrible sense of foreboding.

Then no one spoke as the game progressed.

When they finally came to the grotto, the silence was

broken by the voice of the computer, making even Darren raise his eyebrows in surprise.

This is the resource centre. Here you may choose one object to help you through the Skymaze. At this moment the choices are three: a true sense of direction, the elixir of healing, and the power to defend yourself through menace. Choose wisely. The Skymaze will respond to your choice.

For a moment no one did anything. The sight of the elixir of healing back in the grotto reminded Ben painfully of Mario, confirming beyond doubt that he was now permanently out of the game.

"Go forward," he whispered to Elaine, and her tiny figure moved forward into the grotto. She didn't waste any time. She saw the compass immediately and knew it was what she needed. She moved the joystick and picked it up before Darren had had time to look at the three objects.

"Hang on," he said, "I might have wanted that!"

"Too late now, isn't it?" she retorted. "I've got it."

Perhaps it was because she had moved so swiftly that he automatically did the same; perhaps it was because her competitiveness had flicked his pride and he was really annoyed with her; but before Ben could warn against it, Darren's figure had leaped forward and picked up the third object: black, like the gun, it might have been a weapon or a wand.

"No!" Ben shrieked. "Don't take that! Take the flask!"

But it was too late. There was a moment of silence. Then the computer said gently: *You have now activated the Skymaze. You have also chosen to activate the Dark Clouds.*

Darren moved the joystick to continue playing, but the screen and the figures remained immobile.

After a few seconds they faded, and across the bottom of the familiar cliff top ran the words: STATE OF PLAY: LEVEL 4: SKYMAZE ACTIVATED. PALE GUARDIANS ACTIVATED. DARK CLOUDS ACTIVATED. CONTROL PLAY IMPOSSIBLE

"What happens now?" Darren said, gazing confused at the screen, and moving the joystick to and fro in vain.

"God only knows," Ben said, trying to hide his panic. He deftly pressed the eject button and slipped the disc into his pocket. They had got the compass, but what else had they activated? He and Elaine gazed in silence at each other. Her face was pale and she was chewing her lip.

"Weird game," Darren said, standing up and stretching. He was unusually pale too, and he was frowning as though he was trying to work something out. "It looked as if it should have been much better. How d'you play the next level?"

"We've got to get back to school," Ben said, evading the question.

Darren studied them thoughtfully as they left the room. "I'll find out," he called threateningly after them. "You see if I don't!"

"He won't give us away, will he?" Elaine demanded as they left the house. Even as she said it, she found herself wondering if she would really mind all that much. In a way it would almost be a relief to have the choice taken out of her hands. It would make things much simpler if Auntie Jan said she couldn't go to any more rehearsals and she couldn't be in Shaz's show. She wouldn't have to worry about turning up to rehearsals with her foster mum like a little kid, and then she could just go away with her dad at the end of the year, and she

150

wouldn't have to keep worrying about him and missing him. "But then, I'd miss my chance to be famous," she added to herself. "Back to square one!"

"He probably won't," Ben replied. "He'll just use it as yet another thing to hold over me and get me to do what he wants."

"You shouldn't let him," Elaine said indignantly. "That's blackmail! And why didn't you tell him not to take the weapon?"

"I did tell him, but it was too late. Not that it would have made much difference. Telling him not to take it would probably be a hundred per cent certain way of making him take it. That's the way he is. He's always been like that. And they don't call it blackmail when it happens in families."

"It's all about power," he was thinking. "Everyone wants to feel powerful. And making other people do things they don't want to do, or knowing things about them they don't want other people to know, gives you power over them."

He couldn't help remembering the moment in Skymaze when he had acted for himself. He had stood up. He had ended the game. "Darren's going to get what's coming to him," he thought suddenly to himself. "Because we're going to solve the Skymaze!" He didn't know where this certainty came from. On the face of it he should be feeling worse, because activating the Dark Clouds would almost certainly bring extra complications to the game. But he had an inner confidence that everything was going to be all right. He gave Elaine a grin. "We'd better go back to school separately, in case anyone gets the wrong idea!"

CHAPTER ELEVEN

"What do we do next?" Elaine asked Ben as they waited to cross the road after school. No one had said anything about their earlier absence, and they were both starting to relax about it, hoping they had got away with it.

"We've all got to be together to get into the maze," he replied. "Andrew's got a scheme to get his step-father to take us all out somewhere at the week-end. He thinks he can swing it. So don't make any other plans. I'll tell you tomorrow. I'm going to go and phone him now."

"I just hope I'm allowed to go," Elaine said doubtfully.

"Andrew's going to get Dr Freeman to do all the asking. That way the oldies are bound to let us go! Dr Freeman and Dad had a long conversation the other night, about young people needing more adult supervision and more father figures, and they both agreed they would try to spend more time with us. So now's their chance!"

"I wish we could do it all sooner," she said grimly. "Get it over with and get back to normal." She didn't say, "What about Mars?" but they were both thinking it.

"Don't worry too much about him," Ben said after a pause. "He'll be all right."

She nodded and tried to smile, not very successfully. "Oh well, I'll see you tomorrow. I'd better go, I'm supposed to be walking straight home."

She was dutifully doing this when she saw Linda waving to her from the other side of the road. They had not spoken since their disagreement and Elaine was pleased to be able to make up, though she realised rather guiltily that she had hardly thought about Linda at all—she had been too preoccupied with all the other things going on in her life.

"How've you been?" Linda enquired tentatively.

"Not bad. Yourself?"

"Not bad." Neither of them said, "Sorry", but they both felt it, and each felt the other one feeling it. Linda grinned. "Well, come on," she teased, "I can't wait to hear about your great escapade. Staying out all night! What did you do? Where did you sleep? Weren't you scared?"

"How did you hear about it?" Elaine demanded.

"Mrs Fields phoned us up to see if we knew where you were. Mum was terrified. She was sure you and Ben had been abducted and murdered—you know what she's like. If I'm five minutes late back from school she's prowling the streets looking for me!" Then she insisted curiously, "But what *were* you doing?"

Elaine said, sticking to the story she and Ben had cooked up between them, "We couldn't find Darren, so we went and got something to eat while we waited for him, and then we missed the last bus home. We just thought we'd stay up all night to see what it was like." It sounded really lame to her ears, but Linda was impressed.

"Wow!" she said. "My mum would have killed me! Wasn't Mrs Fields furious with you?"

"She was, rather," Elaine said uncomfortably. She was still feeling bad about upsetting the Fields so much, when they were being so good to her. "Sheesh," she thought, "I hate feeling like this! I hate feeling I should be grateful to them all the time. I don't know if I can stick much more of it."

"I'm supposed to be grounded," she said. It was a funny expression. She tried to imagine her father using it, but the whole idea of "grounding" anyone was so foreign to his nature that she gave up. What would he have done, she wondered, if she had stayed out all night while she was living with him? He might have given her a thump, he might have given her a hug, but he wouldn't have "grounded" her!

"Oh, too bad," Linda was saying. "I was going to ask if you wanted to come and sleep at my place on Saturday. Mum said I could ask you and we could get some videos. And she said they'd take us out somewhere on Sunday—we could go to the beach if the weather stays like this."

"I can't really do anything on the weekend," Elaine said. Watching videos with Linda sounded like a nice, normal thing to do—and so completely unlike what she probably would be doing instead. She couldn't help smiling in a sort of rueful amazement, thinking of the compass and the Skymaze.

"Why not?" Linda said inquisitively, not missing the smile.

"Oh . . ." Elaine was going to evade the question, but she could see that Linda was starting to look hurt, and she didn't want them to have another fight. So she told her about the outing Andrew was arranging.

"Oh!" Linda exclaimed. "Do you think I could come

too? I think I'd better," she added, doing a little bit of arithmetic in her head. "There's going to be an awful lot of boys and only one girl—you! I'd better come and give you some moral support!"

"I don't know," Elaine said. "I'll have to ask Andrew." The thought occurred to her that Linda might have a useful role to play. "Do you like Darren Challis?" she asked hopefully.

"Darren Challis? He's at least seventeen!" Linda squealed. Then she said with a giggle, "He's got lovely blue eyes!"

"Lovely blue eyes!" Elaine thought. "Yeah, well, I'd rather have those lovely blue eyes occupied elsewhere, and not chasing after me!"

"Then there's Andrew's stepbrother, Paul," she told Linda. "I don't think he's very nice, but you never know, he might be your type!" Then she wished she hadn't mentioned Paul, for the memory of the first and last time she had seen him in the Skymaze sent a chill through her, making her suddenly lonely and afraid.

"Do you want to come in for a bit?" she asked Linda when they got to the gate. "I'm not meant to be seeing anyone, but Auntie Jan probably won't mind since she reckons you're such a good influence on me."

"Okay," Linda agreed. "I'll have to phone Mum, though."

However, before the two girls had got to the front door, it opened, and Mrs Fields stood before them with a look of great displeasure on her face.

"You had better go home, Linda dear," she said briskly. "I'm afraid I have something rather serious to talk about with Elaine."

"What's she done now?" Linda couldn't help asking. Mrs Fields did not reply. "Inside, missie!" she said to Elaine. "Goodbye, Linda!"

Standing inside the house, which always seemed dark and stuffy, Elaine thought rebelliously that nothing she had done warranted being called "missie"!

"Come into the kitchen, Elaine!"

She followed the older woman in, and sat down at the table as she was told to. For a couple of moments they stared at each other. Then Elaine gave a theatrical sigh and demanded, "What am I supposed to have done?"

"One of the teachers from my school lives opposite the Challises in Forsyth Avenue. Does that make you realise what you've done?"

"Teachers!" Elaine thought furiously. "Always spying on you!" She tried to brazen it out.

"I still don't understand," she said, trying to sound innocent.

"This particular teacher," Mrs Fields went on, "was home today with the flu. She says she saw you and Ben go up to his house just before lunch, and spend an hour or so there. I just want you to tell me if that is true or not."

Elaine's first instinct was to react as if she was being falsely accused. She was even opening her mouth to say that of course it wasn't true and how could people make up such stories—it must have been someone else, she wasn't the only red-headed girl at Fernleigh—but the sight of Mrs Fields' concerned, kind face stopped her. She just couldn't bring herself to tell any more lies.

"We did go to his house," she admitted. "But we weren't doing anything wrong. He had a new computer game he wanted to show me."

"You deliberately left school to play computer games?" Mrs Fields sounded as if she could not believe it.

156

"I can't concentrate on anything anyway," Elaine replied sullenly. "I can't stop thinking about Mario."

"I'm very sorry about what happened to Mario, but can't you see, I don't want the same sort of thing happening to you. I don't want you getting into trouble, or danger. You have got to learn to keep the rules we set for you. I don't think they're unreasonable—they're for your own protection. Don't you understand that?"

"You don't understand," Elaine returned. "You don't understand about anything!"

"Well, love, please try and tell me. I *want* to understand."

"But I can't," Elaine thought. "How can I explain that the rules don't apply to Skymaze? It has its own rules!"

"I'm waiting for some kind of explanation," Mrs Fields said rather sharply when she did not answer.

But Elaine still could not think of anything sensible to say. "I'm sorry," she said weakly.

Mrs Fields was not at all placated by this. "I'm afraid being sorry isn't enough," she said. "You have to learn not to do it again. So you will phone this Shaz person and tell her you will not be able to be in her show. I imagine the Challises will say the same for Ben."

Now that the decision had been made for her, Elaine realised strongly that it was not the one she wanted at all. "No!" she said furiously. "You can't do that! Please don't do that! I've got to be in it. She wants me to be in it. I'm one of the best people she's got."

"I'm really sorry about it," Mrs Fields replied. "I know how much it means to you. But we said you were on your last chance, and you overstepped the bounds. You have got to take responsibility for that."

Elaine stared at her, hurt and angry. To her rage she could feel tears coming to her eyes. She bit her

157

lip furiously, determined not to cry. "You're not sorry, you're glad!" she shouted. "You never wanted me to do the show, and now you're glad you've got an excuse to stop me. Well, stuff it, then! Stuff the show! Stuff the lot of you!" Then she ran out of the room.

When she got to her bedroom she sat down miserably on the bed and gazed around. "It's not *my* room," she thought. "I'm just being allowed to live here." It was attractively furnished in a rather basic way, but Elaine had had no say in choosing the colours or the materials. It was just how it had been when the last of the Fields' foster children had left home. Elaine couldn't help thinking of Linda's bedroom, where all the treasures she had collected since babyhood were lovingly displayed. "I don't own anything," she thought angrily, looking around at her pitifully few possessions. "All I've got is myself—and now they're telling me what I can and can't do with me!"

From the dressing table the panda Mario had given her looked sadly back at her.

She must have been sitting there brooding for about half an hour, when Mrs Fields knocked gently on the door and called through it, as though nothing had happened, "Time for your gym class, Elly!"

"I'm not going!" Elaine shouted back.

"Now don't be silly!" Mrs Fields said, opening the door and coming in. "Good heavens, you aren't even changed. You'd better get a wriggle on!"

"I thought I was supposed to be grounded," Elaine muttered, not moving from the bed.

"That doesn't apply to gym classes. You've made a commitment there, you must keep going till the end of the year."

"Well, I'm not going to," Elaine said stubbornly.

She knew she was only hurting herself, but it gave her a painful feeling of satisfaction. At least she was the one doing the denying, and not some outsider.

Mrs Fields looked at her for a moment, and then said seriously, "You know I can't force you to go. I don't think it's a very sensible decision, but you must decide for yourself." Then she went out of the room again and closed the door.

Elaine sat there feeling silly. She wished she could call out that she had changed her mind, but she just couldn't bring herself to. She was really sorry about it too—she felt as if she needed the release from tension that physical activity always gave her. She took off her school uniform and put on an old tank top and sports briefs. Then she put on the "La Bamba" tape as loud as it would go. The music filled the room, and she began to dance wildly and bitterly, trying to concentrate so hard that she could not think about how difficult life had suddenly become.

"What the heck do you mean, Darren picked up a weapon too?" Andrew was so horrified he forgot he was trying to be quiet. He looked nervously round the hallway and then hissed down the phone, "Whatever happened?"

"He came in while we were playing the game and forced us to let him have a go." Ben's voice sounded uncannily distant and electronic. "He said he'd dob us in if we didn't. And then—he took this new object before we could do anything about it." There was a pause, and then he said apologetically, "I'm afraid it's activated another level. It's gone up to Level Four, and some things called Dark Clouds are activated now too."

"Oh, nice one!" Andrew said in despair. "The last

thing we want is your crazy brother getting in the way! Suppose these Dark Clouds act on him the way the Pale Guardians have taken hold of Paul? Couldn't you have stopped him somehow?"

"I don't know what else I could have done," Ben replied.

Andrew just prevented himself from saying, "Typical!" Instead he said grumpily, "Well, you'll have to take care of him on Saturday, that's all. Though it might be safer if he wasn't around. Keith's going to phone your dad tonight with his idea for an outing for us all. Do you think you could persuade Darren not to come?"

"Darren's awfully hard to persuade. The best way would be to beg him to come, and then he almost certainly wouldn't—but then Dad would think I really wanted him to, and try to make him!"

"Sheesh!" Andrew groaned. "Why do people have to be so complicated!"

"Yeah, it is rather warm for September, isn't it?" Ben said.

"What?!"

"Someone's here," Ben said guardedly.

"Call me later then," Andrew said abruptly, and put the phone down.

He spent the rest of the evening dashing to the phone every time it rang, until finally, at about eight o'clock, it was Ben again.

"All clear now! How're things your end?"

"Okay for the moment," Andrew said. "All glued to Channel Two!"

"I had an idea," Ben said. "Darren could be useful after all. You know we have to be running away to get into the maze? We could set up a game of Hunter. He

160

could be chasing us."

"What's Hunter, for heck's sake?"

"It's a game he makes me play with him. That's why Elly and I were running away from him the night we got stuck in the maze. He was chasing us in the car park."

Andrew was silent for a few moments while he considered this plan. "It might be okay," he said slowly. "The only trouble is, he'll be able to follow us in this time. It'll mean going through the maze with him after us, as well as Paul probably—and we don't know yet what these . . . what were they?"

"Dark Clouds."

"What these Dark Clouds do." They didn't sound too pleasant, Andrew thought; it suddenly seemed very cold in the hallway.

"I've had a thought about Paul too," Ben said. "You know you said your stepfather might take us sailing? If he took you and Paul and whoever else, Elly and I could get into the maze, and then we'd only have Darren after us. You could keep Paul out of the way— as far out to sea as possible."

"But I want to get in it again too!" Andrew was horrified by this suggestion. He still hadn't given up the dream that he was going to be the one to solve the Skymaze.

"I know," Ben said. "But there's nothing special for you to do. We've got the time, and the direction finder. You might be more use on the outside. Besides . . ." There was a moment's silence, as though he had suddenly gone away.

"Are you still there?" Andrew demanded. "Besides what?"

"If something goes wrong this time, at least you'll still be outside. At least someone will know what happened."

Andrew could see the strength of this argument, but he still didn't like the idea at all. "I don't know," he said. "I suppose we could try it. I'll think about it, and if I can't come up with anything better, we'll have to do it your way. After all, we've got to do something as soon as possible; we may never get the chance again."

"What's the news on Mars?"

"Just the same. Keith took me in after school to see him. They thought it might help if one of his friends went in and talked to him. But it didn't make any difference." Andrew could not forget the sight of Mario stretched out on the hospital bed, his face smooth as a sleeping child's, while his parents' faces were drawn with weariness and grief.

Andrew said goodbye to Ben, went and reminded Keith to phone the different families and organise the outing, and then went to bed. But he found it hard to get to sleep. He couldn't stop thinking about Mario, and the same image was behind his eyelids later that night when he woke with a start of fear and the realisation that it didn't matter who was in the maze and who was outside. What mattered was that the maze be solved.

CHAPTER TWELVE

The telephone wires to and from the Freeman residence ran hot for the next couple of days, but by the end of the week everything was settled. Keith phoned the Fields to invite Elaine, and as Ben had predicted, after some initial doubts Mrs Fields said she could go. Graham Challis felt it would be excellent to have an outing with his two sons, and for them to have the opportunity to do some sailing. Linda phoned Andrew and invited herself, and Ben, feeling wretched about John Ferrone, asked if John could be included too. When he mentioned this, it seemed like such a good idea to everyone that they could not think why they had not thought of it themselves.

Ben's father picked Linda and Elaine up on Sunday morning in his Nimbus. Keith Freeman took Andrew and Paul and John in the Lancia. They were all going to meet at Mangrove Bay, where the Freemans kept their boat, the *Anna*.

The Nimbus was loaded with food and drink for a picnic lunch, along with games equipment, frisbees, balls and crab nets, and Graham Challis's binoculars and camera, for he was a keen amateur ornithologist.

However, the young people in the car did not look as if they were set to enjoy themselves. Ben and Elaine looked pale and tense, as though they had slept badly for weeks, while Darren seemed to be simmering with barely suppressed anger and determined to pick a fight with everyone.

"We're never going to use all this stuff," he said scornfully to his father. "I thought the whole point of this outing was to do some sailing."

"We've ended up with seven kids," Graham replied, overtaking a tanker rather daringly on the inside. "That's way too many to take out on the boat, all at once. Keith Freeman's going to give you all a go, in shifts, while I organise games for the rest on land."

Darren groaned in disgust. "What is this, Dad, a Sunday School outing?"

"I think it's going to be fun," Linda said, the only person present who was determined to have a good time. She was sitting directly behind Darren, and she leaned forward and smiled sweetly at him. He gave her a look of utter amazement, and groaned again. Elaine and Ben looked at each other and sighed.

"That means he likes you," Ben whispered, with assumed cheerfulness.

"Are you sure?" Linda whispered back, not very convinced.

"Did anyone check the weather?" Darren demanded, gazing sourly out of the window towards the coast. "Because there are some very black clouds over there!"

"They'll blow over," Graham said optimistically. "The forecast was for a fine, mild day."

The clouds did not blow over. They remained banked up ominously in the south-west, and when the

Challises and Elaine and Linda got out of the Nimbus at Mangrove Bay they found that the wind had strengthened. Keith, who had arrived a few minutes earlier, was casting a professional eye over the waters of the Gulf, which were starting to fleck with white.

"Damn," he muttered. "If this gets any worse, it'll be too rough to go out with beginners."

"Aw, Keith," Andrew exclaimed. He wanted his stepfather out of the way. "That was the whole point of coming. It's not too bad, we can go out. Everyone's really been looking forward to it."

"I have!" John put in enthusiastically.

"Okay," Keith said. "I'll take you for starters, and Paul had better come with me. I'll need someone with a bit of experience. That is, unless any of the rest of you have done any sailing."

"I have," Linda said. "We've got a shack on Lake Bonney, and I've been sailing ever since I was a little kid." She was thinking it would be fun to go with Paul. She had made a swift assessment of the boys on the expedition, and had decided that he was the one she liked most—he looked really interesting, sort of dark and brooding, and he was more the right age. Boys her own age really were much too immature, so that ruled out Andrew, Ben and John, and Darren was a bit too old, despite his dishy blue eyes.

"Righto," Keith said, smiling at her. She looked very pretty with her blonde hair pulled back in a ponytail. "A perfectly normal teenager," he thought. "And some of these other kids have such problems!"

"I'd rather go next time round," Paul said suddenly, looking searchingly at Andrew, who, he had just realised, was not included on the first trip.

Andrew sighed inwardly. "This is probably the most heroic thing I've ever done," he thought, "and no one's

165

ever going to know anything about it!"

"Can I come too?" he said, trying to sound eager.
"You can fit in the four of us, can't you?" He
exchanged a meaningful look with Ben, and they
nodded at each other.

Paul said, "You can go instead of me."

Andrew gave him a brilliant smile. "I think we
should go together, learn to co-operate and all that.
Isn't that what this is all about?"

"Sounds like the right spirit," Graham Challis
agreed. "I think I'd like you and Ben to go together
too, Darren."

"I suppose that means being last as usual," Darren
remarked.

Paul seemed to be still hesitating. Andrew winked at
him. "Don't veto!" he grinned.

"That's settled, then!" Keith did not want any more
arguing, or they would get no sailing at all.

"It's all up to you now," Andrew whispered to Ben
and Elaine as the others climbed on to the boat. "For
heaven's sake, don't mess it up!"

Beyond the yacht marina was a reserve with a giant
adventure playground, usually a favourite picnic spot,
but today practically deserted. The steel structures
that supported the giant slides and helter-skelters were
as grey and unfriendly as the lowering sky, and the
wind was starting to whistle and howl around the
maze and the tunnels. As Ben and Elaine, along with
Darren and his father, watched the *Anna* put out
to sea, a few drops of rain blew into their faces. They
could see the life-jacketed figures of the four children
listening seriously to whatever Keith was saying to
them. Graham turned to the contingent left on land.
"What do you lot want to do now? Anyone fancy a

166

game of something?"

"Let's play on the equipment," Ben suggested. Darren made an expression of disgust. "Pretty childish, isn't it?"

"We could play Hunter on it," Ben said casually.

For a moment he thought Darren was going to dismiss this suggestion with equal disgust, but then something clicked with him. Ben could see it in his eyes.

"Okay," he said. There was a sinister edge to his voice that made Ben shiver. "All the better," he thought to himself. "We've got to be really frightened by him. He's really got to make us run away."

"Sounds great fun," Graham said heartily. "You can do that while I take a stroll down to the mangroves. We'll play some organised games later."

"We hope," Ben said aside to Elaine. He could feel her shivering next to him, partly from the cold wind and partly from apprehension.

"Be careful, then," Graham said, "and don't get in the way of other people. Though I don't think there'll be many of them around today!"

As their father walked away, Darren turned to Ben, his eyes bright with menace.

"I haven't forgotten what happened last time we played," he said softly. "You're not going to disappear again. You got me into a heap of trouble last time. I know there's something weird going on, and it's got something to do with that computer game, hasn't it? That game we were playing last week?"

He was much bigger than either Ben or Elaine, and he seemed to have increased in menace, as though the character he had played in the computer game had already started to take him over.

"Don't know what you're talking about," Elaine replied boldly.

"Give us a couple of minutes to get away," Ben said, trying to act as though it was just a friendly game of chasey that they were embarking on.

"Yeah, I'll count to a hundred with my eyes shut," Darren replied sarcastically. "Well, get on with it. Disappear!"

Ben and Elaine began to run towards the largest structure, and as they reached the ladders that led up to the slides, the older boy started in pursuit. The game had begun.

In the adventure playground two long stormwater pipes made tunnels that emptied out at the entrance to a complex wooden maze. Ben and Elaine were creeping stealthily through one of them when they heard a rustle at the end, and the light darkened as Darren jumped into the pipe ahead of them. They turned frantically and began to scrabble back again, crouching low.

Emerging from one pipe, they immediately turned and ran into the other one. The game was taking hold of them, and they could both feel their pulse beats accelerating with excitement and fear—not only fear of the person pursuing them, but a deeper and more complex fear of what lay ahead if the Skymaze opened up before them, and, even worse, what lay ahead of them all if it didn't.

As they came out of the second tunnel with Darren close on their heels, Ben had a moment of complete terror that they were going to be caught, caught too soon, with no chance of getting into the Skymaze again. In a swift insight he let the terror overwhelm him, and even added to it old fears from the past, from all the former games of Hunter, from childhood nightmares, all the things they had acted out with Shaz. He let them all take hold of him at once. And then he ran. Elaine was right at his heels as they reached the ladders and began to climb. He thought he might have screamed, but at the same moment Elaine gave a sobbing shout of triumph; and he realised they were climbing through darkness. The steel structure they should have been climbing on had disappeared. He felt some different substance forming under his feet, glimpsed the rapidly changing sky, and was dazzled by the huge stars. On his wrist a sudden piercing coldness announced the presence of the unlimited time watch.

Elaine was already leaping upwards. He watched her cling to a strand of the maze and disappear into the sky. He looked back swiftly. Through the dark tunnel he could see Darren, as he had seen him once before at the quarry, but this time Darren was not looking around him in bewilderment: He was looking straight ahead, his face contorted in an alarming expression of wicked and gleeful realisation.

"He can see me!" Ben thought in dismay. "He's coming after us." Without a moment's hesitation he leaped for the strand too, following Elaine up into the first level of Skymaze.

Elaine was waiting for him, and as soon as she saw him, she waved her hand triumphantly. Strapped to her wrist on a dully gleaming metal band was a glass-faced dial.

"I got it!" she exclaimed. "Come on, nothing can stop us now!"

"Darren's after us," Ben panted, taking a breather while he studied the compass. It had a needle, like the one on an ordinary compass, which oscillated between two poles, one marked by a deep blue arrow head and the other by a fiery red one.

"How does it work?" he started to say, but a noise from below made them both jump.

"Let's get out of here!" Elaine said grimly, and they began to climb the ladder.

It soon became clear how the compass worked. When they were heading in the right direction, the needle swung towards the blue arrow, and when they were off course, it swung towards the red. It should have made their journey much simpler, and it saved them from having to retrace their steps, so they were at least safe from the Pale Guardians. But the same horrible apparitions that had alarmed them so much the last time they had been in the Skymaze kept threatening them at every turn, looming up before them and confronting them with fears from which they had tried to hide all their lives.

Their progress was slow and halting. Ben could feel terror growing like a tumour in his chest, threatening to choke him. He could not rid himself of the certainty that Darren was going to catch up with them, Darren armed with the black wand-like weapon, keeper of the Dark Clouds.

"What do we do if we get separated?" he murmured to Elaine. They had halted for a moment before climbing a structure like a frozen fountain that shone palely, as if in starlight. "If I'm not with you, I'll probably go the wrong way, and if I can't retrace my steps, what happens then?"

"You'll have to remember the way," she replied urgently. "You must know it, once you've followed it. You just have to let your body remember it! And if you get killed," she shuddered at the thought of being hit by one of the loathsome things that were opposing them, "you'd better just wait on the cliff. That way you can bring the game to an end if . . . if it all goes wrong. And if I get killed too, we can start again together." She did not want to talk about that sort of thing. She began to climb doggedly upwards.

Ben glanced over his shoulder. There was no sign of anyone after them. He was determined not to get separated from Elaine. He looked up to where she was waiting for him, and started to climb. Behind her he could see the convoluted structures of the Skymaze rising and falling like clouds of cumulus and cirrus.

"Now where?" he asked, as he arrived beside her.

The arrow pointed straight ahead, out over an abyss that gaped beneath them. In the distance they could see another structure that rose even higher than the one they were on, but there seemed to be no way across the chasm between.

"We'll have to go down, and then up," Elaine said. "There's a path over there." She turned to it, and the arrow stayed pointing towards the blue.

As they descended the treacherous slope, darkness began to fall, until they could see above them stars appearing in an indigo sky. It grew colder, too, lonelier and more desolate, and when they finally reached the bottom of the chasm they were shivering.

"Now where?" Ben said. He looked anxiously back the way they had come and wondered if he could or couldn't see something or somebody on the dark slopes above them.

Elaine checked the compass. "Up again," she said, pointing towards the next steep climb. She pulled herself up on to the first terraced surface of the silver-grey structure that rose skywards in front of them, drew back in horror as a faint shadowy creature passed in front of her, and then, taking a deep breath, went forward.

They climbed steadily and slowly onwards until they were higher than they had ever been before. Stretching out below them they could see the spirals and branches of the Skymaze gleaming in all shades of cloud colours, from pure white through to dark grey, against the deep blue of the sky. It reminded Ben of photos he had seen of far-flung galaxies, spirals of stars in the vast universe.

It was exhilarating to be so high, and he was almost beginning to enjoy the sensation when, half way up, his horrible feeling that someone was close behind them suddenly became much stronger. He paused for a moment, and tried to listen. Beyond the high-pitched hum that was the continual background noise of the Skymaze, he could hear the occasional distinct sound of someone climbing.

"He's catching up!" he muttered to Elaine.

She turned her pale face towards him. Her eyes were huge and grey, reflecting perfectly the cloud colours around her. She nodded as she too picked up the alien noise, and she began to climb more swiftly.

When they reached the peak, they found that the further side fell away in a sheer drop.

"This is no good," Ben said in alarm. "We're cornered here, we'll never get away in time."

Elaine faced out over the cliff edge, and the arrow of the compass pointed straight ahead into the blue. "This is the way," she said firmly. "We've got to go on!"

A crunching sound came from immediately below them as their pursuer's foot slipped. Ben gasped. "We'd better do something fast!"

Elaine was squinting upwards. "There's something

172

there! A rope or something." She thought she might be able to grasp it if she leaped for it—but if she missed she would plummet downwards.

"Go for it!" Ben shrieked at her. "If I stay here, he'll go for me first. You might have time to get away. Jump!"

In the split second Elaine made the decision to jump, she heard Ben scream.

She couldn't look. She needed all her concentration to get the rope, and then she needed all her strength to hang on to it. It was swinging her upwards and sideways in a wide arc. As soon as she had secured her grip, she peered down. The rope swung her back over the spot where she had been standing a few minutes before. She could see Darren on the peak. The black wand was in his hand and a cloud of darkness was erupting from it. For a second she could not see Ben, but then she glimpsed him on the edge of the darkness. He did not step towards Darren—he could not—but he thrust out his hand as though to grab the wand.

Darren pushed him, almost lazily, off the cliff.

"You bastard!" Elaine screamed, but her words were torn away by a sudden blast of wind. Terror gripped her as she realised she was now on her own. "I can't do it," she thought wildly. "I'll never do it alone." For a moment she considered letting go of the rope, letting herself fall so she could rejoin Ben on the cliff top and they could start out again together, but the task of coming this far again seemed so immense that she did not think she could face it. Then she felt her feet and legs go numb with a bitter cold. The darkness was floating up from below and enveloping her.

Ben reappeared on the cliff top at the start of the Skymaze, furious and frustrated. He swore angrily to relieve his feelings, which were a mixture of shock and rage compounded by a gnawing sense of failure and loss. "Darren!" he thought. "Always Darren!" The Dark Clouds had enveloped him, shrouding him in hopelessness and fear, forcing him to come face to face with everything that terrified him. And he had not given in to them, he had not surrendered to their menace. He had come through them, had challenged Darren; and Darren, his own brother, had pushed him off the cliff.

His rage was getting in the way of clear thinking. He knew he had told Elaine he would wait for her on the cliff top and, if necessary, leave the Skymaze and end the game. "But how am I going to know?" he asked himself. "I might end it at just the wrong moment, just before she solves the maze. And what if Darren catches up with her, and what if she's turned back by mistake?" It seemed to him that he spent a very long time under the stars, asking himself these questions one after another and going round and round in circles; and all the time something was building up inside him until suddenly he realised that the only thing he wanted to do was to have another shot at the Skymaze. If he didn't, it would mean that Darren had put him down yet again (literally, he realised with a painful laugh). Against all sense, against reason, against his own fears, he was going back in.

What had Elaine said earlier? She had told him he could remember the way if he had travelled it before. "My body knows it," he thought. "I've done it before, I must be able to do it again. I've got to be able to. I can find the way back to the place I fell from, and then I can go down the rope like Elaine did. And when I get there, I'll catch up with them. Darren is not going to stop me."

174

He climbed the ladder, and slowly, carefully, concentrating as he never had before, he began to follow the way the compass had led them earlier. He had been through the Dark Clouds. He was no longer afraid. Nothing impeded the sure, certain memory that he had within him.

CHAPTER THIRTEEN

The wind had strengthened and it was raining quite hard. The *Anna* was starting to dip and roll heavily. "We'll have to call it a day!" Keith shouted to Paul.

"Yes, let's get back," Paul replied with strange urgency. He looked from the shore to Andrew, and then stared upwards, trying to pierce the clouds with his gaze. His face was dark and angry.

Andrew had been watching the shore anxiously. He could see no sign of the others, though there was someone strolling casually back along the foreshore who might have been Ben's dad. He looked upwards at the dark sky and shivered, not only from the wind. Something else was making him cold, a memory of the moment the white hands had grasped him, and, just before all consciousness faded, had fed on his deepest and most secret fears. Tension and fear were building up within him. Somewhere up there was the Skymaze, and high in the maze the final drama was being played out.

"Wake up, Andrew!" Keith called to him, as the boom swung back, missing him by centimetres. "You'd better stop daydreaming and help Paul get the sail down."

"I'll do it!" Linda said. She made her way carefully towards him and grinned at Paul as she shook the rain out of her eyes. He did not grin back at her, however. His eyes were fixed on Andrew.

"You come over here, John!" Keith ordered. "Hold the wheel steady for me for a moment." As John took the wheel, Keith asked with a smile, "Enjoying yourself?"

"It's ace!" John said, his eyes shining.

Keith had swung himself across to give Linda a hand when the boat yawed, the sail whipped and smacked, and the boom cracked across. Someone gave a shout, and when Andrew looked around he saw Paul in the water, swimming rapidly towards the shore. Andrew didn't think twice. With a cry of rage he dived off the edge of the boat after him.

He caught up with him about a hundred metres from the shore, where the water was still too deep to stand. By grabbing the back of his waterlogged sweater, he was able to make Paul stop.

"Let go, you idiot," Paul yelled at him, kicking and struggling. The water was dark and opaque, and tasted vile.

"Where d'you think you're off to?" Andrew gasped, spitting out a mouthful.

"They're in it, aren't they? I can feel it. They're in the maze again. Someone's getting close to the centre. I've got to stop them." He put his hand on Andrew's head and tried to push him under the water. Andrew retaliated by grabbing wildly at one of Paul's ears and twisting it. Paul let go of him with a shout of rage. Then he turned and tried to swim again, but Andrew held tightly on to the buckle of his life-jacket. He could hear someone yelling from the boat, but he was determined not to let go. Nevertheless, little by little,

177

Paul was pulling them both closer to the shore.

Elaine was clinging terrified to the rope. From where Darren still stood below her on the cliff top, holding the wand, the dark clouds floated upwards, and each time she swung back through them, they reached higher around her, turning her limbs to ice so she could not move. It seemed that it would be only a matter of time before they reached her hands, and then she would have to let go of the rope and fall to her death.

But then, as she swung back away from Darren, she spotted a tiny platform just below her. If she let go now, at once, she would drop on to it. Without even thinking, she let go. She fell along the edge of the cloud of darkness, crying out in horror as it touched her face. But then she was through it and on the platform, wobbling precariously on her numbed feet. She found her balance and straightened up. Looking back, she saw the rope snake away, and in the distance she could see Darren, on the cliff top, preparing to leap for it.

"Hell," she thought. "Where to now?"

She looked at the compass and tilted it until the needle found the blue arrow. Down. She gulped. There didn't seem to be any way down. She leaned over the edge of the platform and saw that underneath it there were hand-holds. If she swung down, holding them, she could grasp the slender silver pole that supported the platform, and slide down.

It did not look terribly difficult, but when it came to actually doing it, she found that something had happened to her nerve. Something had got inside her mind and was conjuring up images to terrify her. She had a dreadful feeling that she had failed, that she had done something irreparably wrong and blown it forever. There was no point in continuing; she might as well give up now. She had made the wrong choice and had lost everything dear to her. She thought desperately of her father, and it seemed to her that she could see him walking slowly away from her and that she would never see him again.

All these fears she recognised as her own, but now they were joined by others that were not only hers. Someone else was afraid of losing his father, of being pushed to one side, of no longer being loved. "That's Andrew," she said to herself, with an ache of pity. Then into her mind came someone who she knew was Ben, who was afraid of being taken over and destroyed by everyone around him, especially his brother. And there was a faint, chilling suggestion of a deep-rooted fear that belonged to someone who believed that no one had ever loved him and that he would never make it, whose life was over before it had begun. Mario.

"Help me!" Elaine screamed aloud. "I can't do it on my own. It's too hard!"

She crouched on the tiny platform, deep in the heart of the Skymaze, while Darren, swinging above her, let the wand release its deadly cloud again.

"I must go on," she told herself. "I can't just huddle here and wait for it to get to me. If it touches me again, I've had it. I must go on now. It's not only for me, it's for all the others too. They are my friends. We are all on the same side. I've got to do it."

She reached underneath, grasped the hand-holds firmly, and somersaulted carefully over the edge. Then she reached for the pole and clasped it with hands and feet. She began to slide downwards.

As she descended, she realised that she was dropping into the centre of the maze. It stretched in every direction around her, and now that she was at the centre, she could see its perfect symmetry. She marvelled at its beauty and complexity as it curved around her like the inside of a glass globe, shimmering and almost translucent.

It was so beautiful that her fears would have left her if she had not glanced up to see that Darren had dropped on to the platform and was crouched down on it, pointing the wand over the edge towards her. Terror swept over her again, and she let herself slide down faster, until her hands burnt from the friction and the Skymaze shot past her in a blur.

"I'm going too fast," she thought in panic. "I'm going to get killed when I hit the bottom. Then I'll have to start all over again." She groaned aloud, gripped the pole with all her strength, and slowed herself down a little.

She still hit the ground hard, hard enough to wind her for a moment. She shut her eyes, terrified that when she opened them again she would find herself back at the start, but when she dared to look, she saw that she was at the entrance to a small, formal maze with silvery walls. Above and around her, in all directions, stretched the Skymaze. She looked upwards at the pole. Darren was half way down it, and tendrils of darkness were already snaking towards her.

Elaine looked back at the compass. The needle spun around until it found the blue pole. Following it, she entered the maze within the maze. Once inside, she began to run.

Twisting and turning according to the leading of the compass, she took no notice of her own reflection on the silver walls running as though eternally through the puzzle, but a couple of times she saw other reflections, the dark shadows that heralded her pursuer, and these made her try to speed up. She was staggering now, exhausted by fear and slowed down by a terrible loneliness. She felt as if she was the only person left in the world, apart from Darren, who was going to catch up with her and take away everything she most wanted before destroying her. Only the compass, heavy on her wrist, the arrow staying faithfully in the blue pole, gave her any comfort or hope, and so she kept going until she knew there was no choice. She could not turn back because of the Pale Guardians. If Darren and the Dark Clouds caught up with her she would be completely overwhelmed by fear. She had no choice but to find the centre.

And then she stumbled and slipped round one final twist, and she was there. The maze opened out into a circle paved with a shimmery material the colour of the sky at dawn. In the centre of the circle was a small opening from which light streamed. But as Elaine started towards it, shadows darkened one of the entrances into the maze. She could see the silhouette of the wand. Shuddering as the dark clouds billowed towards her, obscuring the centre of the circle and blocking out the light, she ducked rapidly sideways under cover again.

Darren had emerged on the other side and she could no longer see the centre she must reach. He could stand there forever and guard it. She tried to judge the distance between where she stood and the centre, but she could no longer see it clearly, and the thought of having to go through the Dark Clouds to reach it turned her bones to water. And she could not turn and retrace her steps. The memory of the white hands clutching her nearly made her faint. She froze, immobile and hopeless.

Darren was walking stealthily across the circle, checking each of the entrances to the maze in turn, letting the darkness from the wand flow down each of them. It would only be seconds before he came upon her, and still she could not move. Then, to her amazement, she heard a voice that jolted her out of her paralysis.

"Elly!" it yelled. She knew instantly it was Ben. "Go! Now!"

With chilling swiftness Darren disappeared down one of the paths.

Elaine came alive in an instant. Although she could see nothing, she knew where the light was, beyond the clouds of darkness. Her desperation gave her power and courage. Flinging herself forward, she somersaulted through the Dark Clouds. She felt the full force of all the combined fears, and she thought she was turning to ice, but she landed with her hands around the opening in the centre of the circle.

The hum of the Skymaze ceased abruptly, and into the silence a voice spoke: *The Guardians have failed to guard the Skymaze. They are now inactivated.* The darkness began to lift and the light streamed again. Then Elaine heard, deep in her own mind, a voice that spoke to her alone.

It said simply, "Look."

She thought she would be dazzled by the light, but she could see down through and beyond it. Far, far below her, like a jewel on dark blue velvet, something was spinning and shining. It was blue too, but lighter than the velvet, and streaked most beautifully with white, with a shimmer of green. She reached out for it with a cry of delight, wanting to take it in her arms and cradle it tenderly. It filled her with an intense and passionate love. It was the most beautiful, most perfect thing she had ever seen.

"What is it?" she whispered, and the voice in her mind replied, "You know."

182

It seemed to her that she did know, that she had always known, though she had no idea where the knowledge had come from. She knew it was the Earth, Gaia, the mother of them all, the mother who would never abandon any of her creatures. And she knew also that they were all part of the Earth, no part more important than the others, and that their interdependence was the Earth's life, their disunity its death.

This was the secret of the Skymaze, discovered through skill, co-operation and courage. This precious vision was the reward.

She should have been ecstatic, and in a way she was, but there was still something missing. "The others should be here," she thought with regret. "They should be seeing it too."

Then she remembered Ben. She looked reluctantly away from the spinning Earth and back towards the maze she had come through. The Dark Clouds had gone, and Ben was walking quietly out from one of the entrances. His face was pale and calm. He smiled at her.

Saying nothing, she gestured to the opening in the centre of the Skymaze, and he knelt beside her and looked.

They could have looked at it forever, but the opening was getting smaller, closing up, taking away the vision.

They both heard the same voice inside their heads.

The game is over, it said. *Congratulations. Goodbye.*

Then it added, as though to apologise for its curtness, *It is advisable to hurry*.

Elaine was quite sure she was unable to hurry, but when she got to her feet, she realised she had to. The Skymaze was shrinking. Moment by moment it was getting slowly but unmistakably smaller. She looked anxiously at the compass, and the needle flickered at her as if it was winking. The blue of the arrow head that had led her to the centre of the maze had changed to green, the same green that shimmered through the vision of the Earth. It stood for life and home, and she was going to get back to them both.

"Come on," she said to Ben, her voice echoing strangely through the silence.

"I'd better get Darren," Ben said. "He's back in the little maze. You deactivated him when you got to the centre."

They both hurried back into the silver maze, noticing with some alarm that it was already much smaller and narrower. When they found Darren, he was no longer carrying the wand, and Elaine thought he looked different in some way.

"He's shrinking too!" she exclaimed.

Ben was speechless with amazement.

"Serves him right!" Elaine said in satisfaction. "Shall we just leave him here? We could, you know," she said severely to Darren. "You deserve it!"

Ben shook his head, smiling. He ran to his brother and gave him a hard shake, noticing that Darren was nothing like as tall as he had been. "Come on!" he said. "Get with it! We've got to get out of here!"

Although they were not there, the others who had played Skymaze saw the vision too. Andrew, surfacing one more time through the murky waters of the Gulf, coughing and spluttering, saw a flash in the sky, followed by an insight into something strange and mysterious that he only half understood but that he knew he would never forget. "Oh help!" he thought. "I'm having visions. I must be drowning!" Then he remembered that he was wearing a life-jacket, and he realised that Paul was no longer trying to push him under. He shook the water out of his eyes and looked around. The *Anna* was about fifty metres away. They had got the sails down and the engine was running. Keith was yelling something at him. He sounded angry. Andrew waved to show him he was all right, and looked around for Paul, who was treading water a little way away from him, looking half-drowned.

"Sorry!" Paul said with an embarrassed grin.

"It's all right," Andrew said. All animosity towards Paul had dissolved. "I know it wasn't your fault!"

"It's over now, isn't it?"

"I reckon."

"Well, we'd better go in! You don't need life-saving, do you?"

"No, I can make it!" Andrew replied.

They swam companionably side by side to the shore, where Keith was quite impartially furious with them both.

In Ward 5A of the Children's Hospital, Mario opened his eyes and looked at his brother, Frank, in astonishment. "What are you doing here?" he demanded.

Then he sat up and looked around. "What am *I* doing here?" He looked at his family surrounding him, and saw the joy slowly dawn on their faces. He felt a goofy smile begin to spread across his own. "Hey, don't cry," he said. "I was having the weirdest dream!" Then he allowed his mother to hug him.

Back on the cliff top, Ben was gazing upwards in amazement. The strands of the Skymaze were twisting and shimmering above his head. It looked as though the sky itself was about to fall, as though the whole universe was contracting inwards to the one point

185

where he was standing. A muffled shout came from above his head. "Help! help! I'm stuck!" Then there was a sort of *pop!* and Elaine came slithering down one of the strands of the maze and landed on the cliff top. Darren followed her, without any difficulty, since he had now shrunk so much that he was smaller than she was.

"Look!" Ben said to Elaine, pointing up towards the falling Skymaze.

Elaine gave it a quick glance, but she was more concerned with getting out. "Come on," she said. "We must hurry. We'll be stuck in here otherwise."

"What are we going to do about Darren? We can't take him out like that!" Ben said. "Everyone's going to notice!" Then he couldn't help himself. Looking at Darren, he began to laugh hysterically. "It's the funniest thing I've ever seen! If only you could see yourself!"

"Stop laughing, you moron!" Darren had not spoken while they had been finding their way back through the shrinking Skymaze, and now his voice set them off laughing again. It was high and squeaky as though he had been at a balloon gas cylinder. It was hard to believe he had ever been threatening.

"I bet you're sorry now, aren't you?" Ben went on, enjoying the unfamiliar sensation of being bigger than Darren. "I bet you're sorry you were such a bully to us. It's all your own fault! You'd better apologise. And promise never to hassle us again."

"Okay, okay, I'm sorry," Darren said. "Now do something about me."

"You promise you'll never ever make me play Hunter again?"

"We haven't got time to do anything," Elaine said urgently. "We must get out."

186

"Not till he's promised," Ben said stubbornly.

"I promise," Darren squeaked rather hysterically, shrinking a little more as he said it. "No more Hunter! Now get me out of here!"

They looked around. The sky and the cliff top were much smaller. It was no longer like being out on the edge of the universe, it was more like being inside a small and very claustrophobic bag. They could see that the opening was getting smaller too. Without any more discussion, they made a dash for it. Ben went first, because he was now the biggest, followed by Elaine. Darren did not even have to duck to pass out through the tunnel.

The wind and rain hit them in the teeth as they stepped out on to the top of the highest slide at the playground. Behind them the Skymaze continued to contract and shrink until Ben stretched out his hand and caught something that flashed silver as it spun downwards.

"Here," he said, holding it out to Elaine and shouting against the wind. "This belongs to you."

They stared at it as it lay on her palm, all its complexity condensed into a silver medallion about five centimetres in diameter.

"Wow!" she breathed. "Beautiful, isn't it?"

For a moment the three of them stood there, united in some curious way by the Skymaze. "We did it," Ben thought. "We did it together, and there's the proof of it, lying on Elaine's palm, so perfect and lovely. And for the first time in my life I got the better of Darren, and he's never going to be able to bully me again." He shivered as he remembered the things they had been through, and the terrors that had been awakened. He checked his mind out gently: they had all been laid to rest, and though he knew he would certainly be frightened of other things in his life, he also knew that he was less likely to be intimidated. He thought about his brother. If Darren had not been Darren the game would not have been anything like as exciting, he realised. It was a curious realisation, one that gave him a completely different perspective on life. He was still trying to come to grips with it when Darren put out a hand and gave him a gentle punch on the shoulder. "Come on," he said. "We'd better go and find Dad."

Ben turned his gaze from the Skymaze to his older brother. "You're getting bigger," he said indignantly. He screwed up his eyes as though he was having trouble with his vision, and when he was seeing straight again, Darren was back to his normal size. "Oh well," Ben thought, giving his brother a gentle punch back again. "I'll catch up with him one day, that's for sure."

CHAPTER FOURTEEN

As an outing, it could hardly have been described as a success. The sailing had had to be abandoned because of the weather, and they had to eat their picnic lunch in the cars. Then, because Andrew and Paul were both wearing rugs and because the rain showed no sign of letting up, Keith and Graham decided they all might as well go home. Both the fathers were slightly discouraged, but everyone else was remarkably cheerful, though Ben and Elaine seemed to be about to fall asleep on their feet, Andrew was shivering with cold, and Paul and Darren looked bemused, in a pleasant sort of way, as though they had been very gently lobotomised.

"Well, who's going with who?" Keith enquired.

John had not said much during the picnic. Out on the boat he had managed to forget about Mario for a little while, but once the sailing was over all his anxieties had come sweeping back again. "Can you drop me off at the hospital?" he asked in a subdued voice.

"I'll come with you," Andrew said hurriedly.

"They'll keep you in too if you turn up like that," his stepfather said. "You'll have to go home and put some dry clothes on first."

189

"Oh yeah, I forgot that! I'll walk down later."
Andrew leaned forward and said to John, "You can
stop worrying. He's going to be all right."

"Why don't we take Linda, too?" Paul said to his
father. "She could come back to our place for a bit, and
we could take her home later."

"Okay," Linda said, highly satisfied.

"Well, at least someone got what they wanted,"
Elaine thought wearily. She had the feeling she ought
to be deliriously happy about something, but she
wasn't. She felt exhausted and strangely shaky. Solving
the Skymaze hadn't really solved anything for her as far
as she could see. "I guess Darren's not going to hassle
Ben so much," she told herself, looking at the two of
them amicably sharing a packet of salt and vinegar
chips, "and perhaps Ben's going to stand up for himself
a bit more. And Andrew and Paul will probably work
things out." At that moment Andrew and Paul were
getting rid of the rubbish with great co-operation by
throwing it at each other before they put it in the bin.
She felt in her jeans pocket for the silver medallion
that Ben had given her. The touch of it comforted her
slightly, but she couldn't see how it was going to change
anything for her.

They departed swiftly. Everyone was in a hurry to
get away. Feeling more and more miserable, Elaine
curled up in the back of the Nimbus. She couldn't think
of anything to say to Ben, but she was grateful, in a
very low-key way, for his presence next to her. Before
they had gone more than a couple of kilometres she
had fallen deeply asleep.

She surfaced through a fascinating and complex
dream, not knowing who or where she was. Ben was
shaking her shoulder and calling to her, but she stared

190

at him for a couple of seconds before she remembered who he was.

"Wake up, Elly!" he was saying. "We're at your place."

She climbed stiffly out of the car. She was aching all over, and her mind seemed to have gone numb. Graham had parked just down from the Fields' place. He hadn't been able to park right outside because there was already a vehicle there, a rather beat-up ute, streaked with red dust up to the door handles. She recognised it instantly with a jolt of delight so strong it hurt. She forgot all about saying goodbye to the Challises, she forgot all about thanking them for taking her out, she didn't even close the door of the Nimbus behind her. She ran to the front door, shouting, "Dad! Dad!" The door flew open, and there stood her father.

"Auntie Jan had phoned him," she told the others, when they all met again around Mario's hospital bed after school the following day. "She was really worried about the way I was behaving, and she thought I needed to see him. And now he's going to stay here, at least till after March; and he thinks I should do Shaz's production."

"It's amazing!" Ben said. "How did you swing it?"

"I told him. I said, this is what I want to do, and this is what I want you to do—I really talked to him and he really listened, and that's never happened with us before—and then he said, 'Okay'!" She was still feeling incoherent about it. "He said he thought it was important for me to do it, and so he was going to give up the other job and try and find something here. 'Course, I had to apologise to Auntie Jan for a whole lot of things, but the funny thing was, once everyone was listening to me, I really did feel sorry for being

191

so difficult. Anyway, I've got till March. After that, who knows!"

"Let's have a look at what the Skymaze turned into," Mario said, swinging his legs over the side of the bed. He was looking surprisingly chipper, even elegant, in his new midnight blue pyjamas.

Elaine took the medallion out of her pocket and gave it to him. They all gazed at it in silence for a few moments.

"Hard to believe it got so lethal, isn't it?" Mario remarked. "It's funny how all these games of yours end up the same way, isn't it, Andrew Hayford? Do you think it's got something to do with your personality?"

"It's got nothing to do with my personality!" Andrew replied. "It's Professor Creepy Ito's personality that's warped, not mine. I've got a good mind to write to him and ask him what the hell he thinks he's up to!"

"Good idea! In fact, I'll write to him. It'll give me something to do. I'm getting bored out of my mind stuck in here."

"I didn't know you could write!"

"Ha ha. Very witty. I shall dictate it to one of my willing slaves. Nurse, take a letter!"

"You can send back the blank disc," Ben said, holding it out.

"Did you run it again?" Andrew demanded.

"Yeah, last night." Ben paused for a few moments while they all waited eagerly for him to go on. "It gave the score—the percentage of the maze explored, the lives we lost, and the number of Guardians activated. Then it printed out the same sort of message as after Space Demons . . ."

"Which you said I imagined!" Andrew put in swiftly.

". . . Congratulations on mastering the game, and

192

to play the next one, return the blank disc to this address." Ben shrugged his shoulders ruefully at Andrew and laughed.

"And I suppose you didn't write it down!"

"Well, as a matter of fact, I did!" He produced a piece of paper, which Andrew grabbed from him.

"This old professor is cunning as well as warped!" Andrew exclaimed when he had read it. "It's a different address from Space Demons. Here you go, Mars! Don't lose it whatever you do!"

"Just do me a favour," Ben pretended to groan. "Don't do it yet. Give us a couple of weeks to recover!"

"What about the medallion?" Mario said, holding it up. "Do we have to send that back too?"

"No, that belongs to the Mad Mouse," Ben said, taking it from Mario. "That's Elaine's now to keep."

And he gave it to her.

Also by Gillian Rubinstein in Mammoth

SPACE DEMONS

Space Demons is a computer game with a difference. Imported directly from Japan, it's a prototype destined to lock four unlikely individuals into deadly combat with the sinister forces of its intelligence.

And, as the game draws them into its powerful ambit, Andrew Hayford, Elaine Taylor, Ben Challis and Mario Ferrone are also forced to confront the darker sides of their own natures.

"A wonderful book . . . there's so much to enjoy and reflect on." *Books for Keeps*

Honour Award Australian Book of the Year
Peace Award for Children's Literature
Winner 1988 South Australian Festival Awards

BEYOND THE LABYRINTH

Growing up seems difficult enough for Brenton. He can't get on with his parents, his younger brother is taller than he is and seems to be overtaking him in every way, and his mother has invited 12-year-old Victoria Hare to stay while her parents are overseas. But in comparison with personal problems, the threat of nuclear annihilation is so overwhelming that Brenton no longer wishes to take responsibility for his actions, preferring to act upon the throw of the dice. Life becomes more complicated when an alien anthropologist arrives to study an ancient Aboriginal tribe who once lived in the area round his home – does she confirm his worst fears?

Catherine Sefton

Irish Trilogy
**STARRY NIGHT
FRANKIE'S STORY
BEAT OF THE DRUM**

Catherine Sefton's moving trilogy shows how the political and social situation in Northern Ireland affects young people on both sides of the divide at critical moments in their lives. Each book considers different viewpoints: the disturbing truth behind the crisis in Kathleen's family (STARRY NIGHT); the trouble encountered by the unconventional Catholic, Frankie, who has a Protestant boyfriend (FRANKIE'S STORY); and finally a look at loyalist Protestants through the eyes of young, crippled, Brian Hanna (BEAT OF THE DRUM).

Cara Lockhart Smith

PARCHMENT HOUSE

From the outside Parchment House looks like any other house. But, home for the orphans of Carstairs and Bungho, it holds dark and sinister secrets. And, like the other orphans in the house, Johnnie Rattle is all alone in the world . . .

Governed by the worthies, the children live a life of drudgery maintaining the gadgets designed to make their superiors more comfortable. But when the 'ultimate' gadget arrives life at Parchment House becomes intolerable. Archibald, a huge and gleaming robot, is programmed to control, discipline and educate the children. But when Archie's cruelty becomes too much for the orphans, Johnnie Rattle has the courage to instigate a rebellion. He risks everything to save the children . . .

In PARCHMENT HOUSE, her first novel, Cara Lockhart Smith has created a nightmare world where good triumphs over evil. It is a wonderfully funny, original and touching fantasy.

Diana Wynne Jones

HOMEWARD BOUNDERS

When They threw Jamie out to the Boundaries, he was at first too shocked and amazed to make much sense of it. He'd been told he could go Home if he found himself in the right world, but life seemed to be a succession of strange countries, some pleasant, most dangerous, where survival was all that mattered.

Little by little, though, Jamie realised that there **was** a curious logic in things – he wasn't the only Homeward Bounder, for one thing, though some, like Ahasuerus and the Flying Dutchman, had been trying to get Home for a very long time.

But Jamie decided to try and do more than that. Together with some other Homeward Bounders he plotted to oppose Them direct, in the fortress which seemed to be Their chief stronghold.

This is a remarkable, powerful story, full of unexpected events and ideas, which absorb and fascinate.

Diana Wynne Jones

A TALE OF TIME CITY

Vivian has been kidnapped! She's sure that Jonathan and Sam have whisked her away to a city of the future. But Time City exists outside time and space – though its inhabitants, as Vivian discovers, couldn't be more human.

Trying to get back home, Vivian becomes entangled in the plight of the crumbling Time City. A desperate hunt begins through time to find its builder, the legendary Faber John, and his four precious caskets. But someone else is determined to find him first – someone who is spreading chaos throughout history in an attempt to destroy the city. Is it the dreaded Time Lady? Or an unknown adversary?

A Selected List of Fiction from Mammoth

While every effort is made to keep prices low, it is sometimes necessary to increase prices at short notice. Mammoth Books reserves the right to show new retail prices on covers which may differ from those previously advertised in the text or elsewhere.

The prices shown below were correct at the time of going to press.

☐	416 13972 8	**Why the Whales Came**	Michael Morpurgo	£2.50
☐	7497 0034 3	**My Friend Walter**	Michael Morpurgo	£2.50
☐	7497 0035 1	**The Animals of Farthing Wood**	Colin Dann	£2.99
☐	7497 0136 6	**I Am David**	Anne Holm	£2.50
☐	7497 0139 0	**Snow Spider**	Jenny Nimmo	£2.50
☐	7497 0140 4	**Emlyn's Moon**	Jenny Nimmo	£2.25
☐	7497 0344 X	**The Haunting**	Margaret Mahy	£2.25
☐	416 96850 3	**Catalogue of the Universe**	Margaret Mahy	£1.95
☐	7497 0051 3	**My Friend Flicka**	Mary O'Hara	£2.99
☐	7497 0079 3	**Thunderhead**	Mary O'Hara	£2.99
☐	7497 0219 2	**Green Grass of Wyoming**	Mary O'Hara	£2.99
☐	416 13722 9	**Rival Games**	Michael Hardcastle	£1.99
☐	416 13212 X	**Mascot**	Michael Hardcastle	£1.99
☐	7497 0126 9	**Half a Team**	Michael Hardcastle	£1.99
☐	416 08812 0	**The Whipping Boy**	Sid Fleischman	£1.99
☐	7497 0033 5	**The Lives of Christopher Chant**	Diana Wynne-Jones	£2.50
☐	7497 0164 1	**A Visit to Folly Castle**	Nina Beachcroft	£2.25

All these books are available at your bookshop or newsagent, or can be ordered direct from the publisher. Just tick the titles you want and fill in the form below.

Mandarin Paperbacks, Cash Sales Department, PO Box 11, Falmouth, Cornwall TR10 9EN.

Please send cheque or postal order, no currency, for purchase price quoted and allow the following for postage and packing:

UK   80p for the first book, 20p for each additional book ordered to a maximum charge of £2.00.

BFPO   80p for the first book, 20p for each additional book.

Overseas   £1.50 for the first book, £1.00 for the second and 30p for each additional book
including Eire thereafter.

NAME (Block letters) ....

ADDRESS ....

....

....